TALISMAN

The TEARS of ISIS

Collect all four thrilling
Talisman adventures!

TALISMAN

THE TEARS OF ISIS

ALLAN FREWIN JONES

Hodder
Children's
Books

A division of Hodder Headline Limited

For Kenneth Douglas Hutton –
my grandfather and my inspiration

A Catalogue record for this book is available from
the British Library

ISBN 0 340 88224 7

Typeset in Baskerville by Avon DataSet Ltd,
Bidford-on-Avon, Warwickshire

Printed and bound in Great Britain by
Bookmarque Ltd, Croydon, Surrey

The paper and board used in this paperback by Hodder
Children's Books are natural recyclable products made from
wood grown in sustainable forests. The manufacturing
processes conform to the environmental regulations
of the country of origin.

Hodder Children's Books
a division of Hodder Headline Ltd
338 Euston Road
London NW1 3BH

'Tremble in dread, thief and interloper: thou art
    revealed.
The Gods that protect these Halls know thy
    name,
Intruder in the resting place of Tathtut III,
Great King of Upper and Lower Egypt.
Thou hast brought down a curse upon thyself
That shall be visited upon thy family
Even unto the hundredth generation.
Thy first-born son shall die,
And so shall all the first-born sons of thy line,
Until the end of days.'

*The curse protecting the Funerary Text of the
Scroll of the Dead, found in the tomb of Hathtut III.
Translated by Lieutenant William Christie
of the 21st Light Dragoons, Luxor, August 1883.*

Prologue

The Valley of the Kings. Egypt.
13 August 1883.

The barren valley was shrouded in the deep shadows of night. The sky was pierced with a thousand points of frozen white fire. And the ancient mountains lay awake, watching and waiting like monstrous, misshapen guardians.

All was silent. There was no wind. The entrance to the old tomb showed black in the cliffside – a deeper patch of darkness in the midnight shadows. It was known by the local people as the Pit of Ghosts.

Suddenly, a flurry of hoofbeats broke the

stillness of the night. Three British cavalry officers galloped their horses down the long valley, shouting and laughing as they rode.

Twenty-year-old Lieutenant William Christie drew his horse to a halt outside the ancient tomb. His fellow officers had dared him to spend a night there and he had taken up the challenge, throwing the dare back at them: 'I'll ride to the Pit of Ghosts at midnight tonight! Who will come with me?'

Two had responded: Lieutenants George Cartwright and Charles Church, both the same age as William, both in high spirits and eager to defy the old legends.

The three men dismounted and secured their horses, wrapping the reins around large rocks to stop the animals from straying. Then they paused at the entrance to the tomb while William struck a match and lit a rag and pitch torch. He smiled, amused to see his two companions holding back, waiting for him to make the first move.

A bleak, chill air struck his face as he stepped inside the tomb. The torch flame flickered, and for a moment William felt a strange unease, but he shook it off and walked to the centre of the chamber.

'We'll build the fire here,' he said, stamping his boot. His eyes gleamed. 'I daresay the ghosts will be glad of the warmth and light.' He let out a laugh that rang around the stone walls. 'Let's make ourselves at home.'

George and Charles followed him in, bearing bundles of dry tinder. Soon the fire was lit and the three men sat on blankets, passing a flask and talking together in loud voices, their rowdy chatter awakening age-old echoes. The time slipped easily away as they laughed and joked together.

William took out his pocket-watch. It was already half-past one. 'The ghosts are dull company tonight,' he said, getting up to stretch his stiff legs.

'Perhaps we scared them away,' Charles suggested with a smile.

'Ghosts!' shouted George. 'You are neglecting your guests!'

All three men laughed.

William relit the torch and wandered past the walls of the cavern. The faint, barely-visible remnants of old paintings could just be made out, here and there, on the stone. Even as a boy, he had been fascinated by artefacts and lost languages. With his posting to Egypt, William had seized the opportunity to explore the temple ruins and study the hieroglyphic texts of the ancient pharaohs.

He crouched to peer closely at a strange, hybrid creature – part crocodile, part leopard and part hippopotamus – painted on a stone in the wall. Further investigation revealed that the stone, which was about half a metre square, was loose, so William took out his pocket-knife and dug at the edges. If he could prize it out, it could be taken back to the barracks – absolute proof that he had won the dare.

'Come over here and help me,' he called to his friends.

His companions joined him and they dug together at the crumbling edges of the stone.

'I can get my fingers around it,' George said after a few minutes. 'Stand back.'

'I think not,' William replied firmly. 'The stone is mine.'

'You're welcome to it,' Charles told him. 'I've no wish to be confronted by such an ugly sight every time I enter my quarters.'

'Then you'd best avoid mirrors,' William joked. He forced his fingers into the cracks, gripped the stone and tugged until it came free and he fell back, clutching his prize.

'There's a small chamber,' said George, peering closely at the wall. 'And something is inside.'

William scrambled up. 'Let me see.'

The others made room for him. He held the torch close to the broken wall and the flickering light revealed an alcove cut into the stone. A small jar lay on its side within. It was about the size of a man's fist. William reached in and carefully drew it out.

The others gathered round him as he stared at the jar. There was a cartouche on the curved belly – the name of a pharaoh carved in hieroglyphics by a scribe long ago. The jar had no lid, and the men could see that there was something rolled up inside.

'What is it?' Charles asked. 'Is it worth anything?'

'Possibly,' William replied. 'It must be thousands of years old.' He carried the jar over to the fire and leant down to examine it in the firelight.

'If it's valuable, we will all benefit from it,' said George.

Charles rubbed his hands together and held them out to the heat of the flames. 'Fair shares for all,' he said to William. 'Shall we be rich?'

'I have no idea,' William answered thoughtfully. 'Be quiet. I'm trying to read the writings.'

George stretched out on his blanket, his arms behind his head. 'Let the great scholar work,' he said, smiling at Charles. 'I shall lie here and think of ways to spend my share of the profit.'

William frowned, trying to remember the meanings of the ancient hieroglyphs.

'So?' George asked after a few moments. 'What does it say?'

'Well . . .' William frowned. 'One of the symbols means "book".' He held the jar closer to the fire. 'And there is another I recognise.' He paused. 'It's the symbol for "the dead".' An odd silence swallowed his words.

William looked up, feeling a sudden chill, as if an icy wind had swept through the chamber. On the other side of the fire, George sat up and he and Charles stared at William through the flames.

William gazed back at his companions uneasily. He felt horribly cold now and moved closer to the fire, noticing that his friends were also drawing in, their faces bleak, their hands reaching forwards for warmth. William stretched out his fingers, almost into the fire. But there was no heat. The flames were cold. He snatched his hand back, startled and alarmed.

He thought he heard voices – whispering voices – coming from the direction of the small alcove. He turned his head to stare into the dark hole, his eyes wide with alarm.

'God preserve us!' Charles murmured. They could all hear the voices now. They could all see the threads of blackness that were oozing from the breach and crawling across the sandy floor. The eerie voices grew louder – an incomprehensible babble of anger and menace.

All three men moved at once, scrambling to their feet, backing away from the sinister opening. William glanced at his companions. He saw that their faces were distorted with fear and felt a cold sweat running down his own face.

The ghastly chorus rose – William thought it sounded like a thousand dead men giving voice to an undying rage. Mesmerised, he watched the crawling blackness reach the fire and snuff it out.

Then, tearing himself away, he snatched up his gear and threw himself towards the entrance. His friends were close at his heels, fighting one another to be free of the tomb.

'The jar is yours!' George shouted to William. 'I want nothing to do with it – or with this vile place!'

'I, neither!' Charles put in, as he reached for his horse.

The horses were whinnying, straining at the reins, their eyes wide and rolling in fear. Wordlessly, the soldiers mounted and rode at a gallop, away from the Pit of Ghosts.

Vengeful voices shrieked on the wind that howled in the riders' wake.

And then there was no wind. The icy stars stared down. The mountains watched and waited in the silence of the night.

William sat in his barracks in Luxor. The fear that had sent him and his friends galloping from the tomb had melted away on their return to town. William had ignored the appeals of his companions to join them in some crowded back-street tavern and carouse the rest of the night away. He had work to do. He wanted to learn the secrets of the ancient jar.

An oil lamp cast a pool of light on to his desk. The empty jar stood to one side. It had contained a thick roll of papyrus pages, which William had carefully withdrawn and smoothed out upon the desktop. They were covered with ancient writings.

Slowly, he had written out a translation of the first page on a sheet of white paper, consulting textbooks when his memory failed him. Now, at last, the translation was complete.

The Book of Passage Through the Halls of the Dead. William stared down at the extraordinary words that he had scribbled on the notepaper.

Away beyond the sharp-edged hills, the sun was rising, but William was too absorbed in his work to notice. The pages contained a sacred text, buried with the dead pharaoh to guide his immortal soul into the afterlife. So essential was this text, that a curse had been placed upon it, so that no one would dare remove it from the tomb.

Thou hast brought down a curse upon thyself that shall be visited upon thy family even unto the hundredth generation. Thy first-born son shall die, and so shall all the first-born sons of thy line, until the end of days, William read. Uneasiness crept into his mind. It was a terrible curse.

William wrestled with his fears. His rational mind told him that this was just the superstition of a long-dead people – uncanny, but powerless. But the terror that had assailed him in the tomb came creeping back, and his hand trembled as he held the sheet of white paper to the flame of his oil lamp and watched it burn.

He stood up, walked to the door and threw it open. The pale blue sky outside was streaked with the amber light of dawn. A trumpet rang out, sounding reveille to rouse the soldiers and, with it, William's fear drained away. 'Feeble-minded superstition,' he whispered to himself. 'The curse means nothing!'

Quickly, he returned to his desk, rolled up the papyrus text and pushed it back inside the jar. Then he stashed the jar at the bottom of his foot-locker, slammed the lid shut and turned to face another hot Egyptian day.

Chapter One

The Elephantine Stone

The Valley of the Kings. Present day.

The Valley lies in a loop of the Nile, some five hundred kilometres south of Cairo; its harsh, burnt-brown limestone cliffs forming a final outcrop of the sprawling, sun-scorched dunes of Ghard Abu Muhariq in the Great Western Desert.

Today, the bright sun shone down into the valley, bleaching the hills and beating down upon the bustle and chaos of the great archaeological excavation. Jeeps bounced along dirt tracks, sending up plumes of dust. The slopes of the hills crawled with men in white galabia robes, wielding picks and shovels, or carrying baskets of rubble up and down the steep inclines. Donkeys moved sure-footedly among the stones, laden with panniers, carrying supplies for the broad encampment of tents and trailers. Everywhere, there was noise – of metal striking stone, voices speaking in English and Arabic and engines struggling in the heat.

A line of local men were carrying baskets of earth away from a recently-opened tomb, cut deep into the hillside. The tomb had been carved into the cliffs at the far end of the western arm of the valley, some distance from the site of most of the royal burials. Inside, the air was still and cool. An electric cable snaked along the sloping corridor, powering bright electric lights.

Four people stood in the tomb: twelve-year-old Olivia Christie and her best friend, Josh Welles – just two weeks her junior – along with Olivia's father, Professor Kenneth Christie of Oxford University, and his assistant, Jonathan Welles, Josh's twenty-year-old brother. The two men were stooping to peer at some wall-carvings.

'Be careful, Josh.' Olivia Christie's blue eyes sparkled in the torchlight. She was tall and slim, with long dark hair and a pale, inquisitive face. 'There might be booby-traps.'

Josh Welles paused for a moment. From under his blond, shaggy fringe he peered down the long sloping passageway of ancient limestone. He pushed his hair out of his eyes.

'Nice try, Olly!' he said. 'But I know the tombs around here weren't booby-trapped.' He called out to the two men. 'It was the pyramids that had all the traps to catch grave-robbers, wasn't it? There aren't any here, are there?'

The professor and his assistant were closely scrutinising a carved cartouche filled with hieroglyphics. The professor seemed not to hear, but Jonathan turned his head and smiled at his younger brother's question. He had the same warm brown eyes as Josh, and the same shaggy thatch of blond hair.

'Usually, you'd be right,' Jonathan said. 'But Setiankhra was a pharaoh with a big secret. And he wasn't prepared to rely entirely on the remoteness of the valley and the Necropolis Guards to defend that secret against intruders – so he added some nasty little devices of his own.'

Olly looked at him. 'How nasty?' she asked nervously. Her comment to Josh about booby-traps had been a joke – or so she had thought. She stared down at the stones beneath her feet. They looked solid enough, but she was beginning to regret her eagerness to come on the guided tour of the recently-excavated tomb.

'Come with me and I'll show you some of them,' Jonathan offered. He looked at the professor. 'Is that OK with you, Professor?'

Kenneth Christie looked up. 'What's that?' He had been so caught up in his discoveries that he hadn't heard a word. Olly adored her father, with his untidy greying hair, dishevelled clothes and half-moon glasses on a cord around his neck, but she did find it a little frustrating when he went off into a world of his own and didn't hear a thing that was said to him.

Jonathan repeated the question.

'Yes, that'll be fine,' the professor said absent-mindedly, already turning back to the wall. 'Some of these writings are very intriguing,' he murmured. 'Third Kingdom – definitely.'

Jonathan led Olly and Josh down to a place where the passageway levelled out. Olly guessed that they must now be at least ten metres under the towering cliffs of the desolate valley. It was an awesome thought.

The walls and ceilings of the passageway were covered in intricate designs – columns of hieroglyphic script and drawings of strange and fabulous beast-men with snake-heads and bird-heads and dog-heads. Jonathan shone his torch at a particular section of the wall. It was pocked with a series of holes. Josh and Olly stepped closer to look. In the torchlight they could see that each of the holes was blocked by something deep inside – something slender and sharp.

'Those are stone spikes,' Jonathan explained. 'If a robber triggered the trap, they'd shoot out and impale him.'

'Wow!' breathed Olly, wide-eyed. 'Are they safe?'

'Of course they are,' Josh said. 'Jonathan and your dad wouldn't let us down here if we were likely to get stone spikes through our heads.' He looked at his brother, his voice a little uneasy. 'That's right, isn't it?'

Jonathan nodded. 'Quite right,' he agreed.

The professor came up behind him. 'Impalement was the preferred method of execution for tomb-robbers,' he said gravely. 'To break into a tomb and steal the grave goods was the worst crime imaginable.' He frowned, shaking his head. 'But someone managed to get in here without falling foul of the booby-traps. This tomb was looted a long time ago – probably within a few centuries of it being sealed.'

Olly looked at her father. 'How would the spikes have been triggered?' she asked, curiously.

'I imagine it would have been a mechanism involving wires and pulleys and counter-balances,' replied the professor. 'It probably won't have been operative for thousands of years.' He pointed across the floor, and explained, 'These stones were placed with great precision. Balanced to tilt at the pressure of a foot and hurl the unwary intruder into a deep pit.'

Olly's eyes widened. She noticed that tapered blocks of wood had been hammered into cracks between the stones.

'Don't worry,' her father assured her. 'It's quite safe as long as no one removes the wedges.'

'But it's not just spikes and pits,' Jonathan added. 'There were enormous stones that would drop from the roof to crush intruders. And poison smeared on door handles and pitchers of toxic powder carefully positioned to fall and break when a door was opened. Not to mention wires stretched across the corridors at neck height, ready to cut a robber's head off.'

Josh and Olly exchanged a nervous glance.

'They had some pretty unpleasant ways of dealing with burglars back then,' Olly remarked.

'They certainly did.' Professor Christie had come to the end of the lights powered by the cable from the electric generator. He unclipped a torch from his belt and switched it on. The bright beam revealed a second long slope which he began to descend.

'I'm going up top for a few minutes,' Jonathan said. 'I've seen a few things down here that I'd like to check up on.' He turned and headed up the passage to the small square of daylight that marked the mouth of the tomb.

Josh and Olly looked at one another.

'I suppose they have found *all* the traps?' Josh said.

'I hope so,' Olly replied. She switched on a torch of her own and hurried down the corridor to catch up with her father.

Josh followed. 'All the same – you won't *touch* anything, will you?' he said to her. 'You know what you're like.'

Olly glanced at him, eyebrows raised. 'Meaning?'

'Meaning, don't go prodding at things without asking your dad first,' he answered firmly. 'I don't want to get squashed flat by a huge great stone, because you've accidentally set off some old booby-trap.'

'I'm not completely daft,' Olly said with a laugh. 'I won't touch a thing. I promise.'

Josh smiled. 'Good.'

Olly didn't really need Josh to tell her to be cautious. The tomb had only been discovered four weeks ago. And it was very big, with at least eighteen chambers. Hardly anything was known yet about the breathtaking, three-and-a-half-thousand-year-old burial site, apart from the fact that it had once housed the mummy of a pharaoh called Setiankhra.

Professor Christie had discovered its location after translating hieroglyphic carvings on a stone he had found on Elephantine – an island in the Nile, known locally as Abu.

Olly had been on several expeditions with Josh, Jonathan and her father, but she had rarely seen the professor so excited as when he had found the Elephantine Stone. The writings on the stone had not only given directions to the lost tomb of Pharaoh Setiankhra, they had also referred to something even more astonishing. The writings indicated that, within the tomb, lay hidden one of the Talismans of the Moon!

This was astonishing because the Talismans of the Moon were the stuff of legend – of film and fantasy. Olly never tired of hearing Jonathan and her father discuss the incredible story attached to them. According to the legend, the Talismans of the Moon had been created in ancient times, by priests from different cultures around the world – priests who all served the moon god, or goddess, of their people. Each of these priests crafted a single talisman. And it was said that if all these talismans were brought together, in the right place, then a great secret of knowledge, learning and time would be revealed.

So went the legend, but the writings on the Elephantine Stone were the first indication that the myth *might* have some basis in reality.

From his research through ancient Egyptian, Assyrian, Greek and Roman texts, Professor Christie had come to believe that the Talismans of the Moon were in fact the key to unlocking the lost

Hall of Records – also the stuff of legend, but a legend which the professor had long believed to be true. If the talismans really opened the Hall of Records, then they could indeed be said to reveal a great secret of knowledge, learning and time – for the Hall of Records supposedly contained a copy of every ancient and magical text of its era.

Since concluding that the Hall of Records really did exist – somewhere – Professor Christie had made it his life's work to find it. And so the possibility that the Talismans of the Moon might *also* exist, had filled him with excitement and had brought him – not to mention Olly, Josh and Jonathan – here, to Setiankhra's tomb in the Valley of the Kings.

Josh and Olly walked gingerly across the wedged, booby-trapped stones and followed the professor down the second corridor. Shadowy chambers opened out on either side, and Olly glimpsed stunning paintings and carvings within them.

The professor paused, pointing the torch towards an odd circular painting. 'That is a picture of the snake that devours itself,' he said. 'It's an ancient symbol of eternity. And around it are the seven stars that the Egyptians called the Krittikas – the

Judges of Mankind. We know them as the Pleiades.'

'Imagine how much work it took to get all this done,' Olly murmured in amazement.

'And then they just sealed the whole lot up and forgot about it,' Josh put in.

'Yes, indeed,' the professor said. 'Scores of workers toiled down here, using only wooden clubs and copper chisels. They laboured day after day for ten years or more. And their only light came from small, flickering oil lamps.' He paused at the entrance to another chamber, shining the torch beam from side to side. To the left, it revealed a life-sized statue of a jackal-headed man with evil, gleaming green eyes.

'Yikes!' Olly exclaimed, startled by the malevolence in the painted eyes. 'Who's he?'

'A shabti warrior,' her father told her. 'The writings here are spells and incantations, intended to bring the pharaoh's magical guardians to life should anyone attempt to break the great seal and enter his burial chamber.'

'Who'd be daft enough to believe that?' Josh queried lightly.

The professor turned and looked at him. 'Never dismiss things, simply because you don't understand them, Josh,' he said. He moved the torchbeam over the square entranceway. 'Not everything can be scientifically explained.'

Olly turned her torch on Josh and saw him staring at her father, looking puzzled. Then she shone the light on the shabti warrior and his chamber. The doors stood wide open and the floor was silted and strewn with debris.

'This is the result of flooding,' observed Professor Christie. 'Every few hundred years this region suffers torrential rainstorms. Millions of tons of floodwater pour into the valley, even seeping into the tombs themselves.' He sighed. 'It's caused immense damage.'

'Are we due one of those storms any time soon?' Olly asked. 'Only, I'd have brought an umbrella.' She looked back up the narrow way they had come – imagining a murderous flood of black water, roaring down to engulf them.

'I think the meteorological people would have warned us,' her father replied with a twinkle in his eye.

'Excuse me,' Josh asked, 'but if this is the burial chamber, where's the sarcophagus?' He knew that the mummified body of the pharaoh, in its gold-encrusted casket, was usually placed within a great hollowed-out stone box – but there was no such box in the chamber.

'That's a very good question,' Professor Christie replied. 'It ought to be in here, but it clearly isn't.'

'Maybe the robbers took it?' Olly suggested.

'It would have been made of granite or quartzite,' her father responded. 'The robbers were searching for gold.' He stepped into the room, running his torchbeam round the lavishly-decorated walls. 'No, I suspect that there's a hidden doorway.' He walked across the uneven floor and stooped to examine some writings. 'There must be a clue here somewhere,' they heard him mutter.

'When my dad finds the secret door and the treasures, he'll be famous!' Olly told Josh delightedly. 'Hey, Dad! I bet there'll be TV programmes about you. And books and computer games – maybe even a Hollywood movie!'

Professor Christie looked at her. 'Good lord, I hope not,' he replied. 'I'd never get any work done with all that kind of nonsense going on.'

'No problem,' Olly assured him. 'I'll do the TV shows for you.'

Her father smiled indulgently. 'I think you're

getting a bit ahead of yourself, Olivia,' he said. 'So far, all I have are riddles and puzzles. It could take years of painstaking research before the secrets of Setiankhra's tomb reveal themselves – if they ever do.'

'Of course they will,' Olly declared with absolute conviction. 'You're a genius, Dad – you'll solve the mystery.'

Her father laughed gently and turned to study the cryptic wall paintings again. 'Just like her mother,' Olly and Josh heard him say fondly.

It was several years since Olly's mother had died in a plane crash, during an expedition to Papua New Guinea. Since then, Olly's gran had accompanied father and daughter all over the world, overseeing the domestic arrangements and acting as a stern but affectionate tutor for Olly and Josh.

Josh and Jonathan's mother, Natasha Welles, was a film star. She spent so much time filming in foreign locations that she was often away from home for long stretches. That was why Josh travelled with his older brother on archaeological expeditions. Besides which, Olly's gran thought it was good for Olly to have someone of her own age around.

Olly looked at her friend. 'Wouldn't it be great if the two of *us* found the secret doorway?' she said. 'I mean, there are only so many walls in here – how difficult can it be?'

Josh looked at her dubiously. 'Pretty difficult, I should imagine,' he replied. 'Besides, it may not even be in here – it might be in one of those other rooms we saw on the way down. If I was hiding something, I wouldn't hide it in the most obvious room in the whole tomb. I'd be sneakier than that.'

Olly looked at him. 'You know, that's not a bad idea,' she said. She shouted to her father, 'Is it OK if we explore some of the other rooms?'

'As long as you're careful,' her father called back.

Olly led the way, raking the floor with torchlight as they headed back up the corridor. They reached a small square chamber. Paintings and writings covered the walls, some still bright and well-preserved, others smeared and stained and fragmented. Olly pointed her torch into the dark corners. Silt was piled against the wall – testament to the ancient floods.

'We should do this scientifically,' Josh said. He pointed. 'Let's start over there and work our way round. We need to look for regular cracks – and parts of the walls that are sunken, or that stick out more than the rest.'

They began to pick their way across the debris left by three thousand years of flood-water. The beam of the torch lit up a stylised painting of a jackal-headed being.

'He looks like that shabti warrior,' Josh said. He glanced at Olly. 'What did your father mean about not dismissing stuff just because you don't understand it? Was he talking about the magic spells?' He gave a crooked grin. 'He doesn't think they might work, does he?'

Olly's eyes gleamed in the torchlight. 'My family is a bit weird,' she replied.

Josh laughed. 'Tell me about it.'

She shook her head. 'No, I mean *really* weird.'

Josh stared at her expectantly.

'I'm not saying I necessarily believe this, right?' she continued. 'But there's a possibility – just a possibility – that there's a curse on my family.'

Josh opened his mouth to laugh, but the look in Olly's eyes silenced him. 'You're kidding me?' he breathed. 'A curse? Really? That's so cool. How did it happen?'

'It started back at the end of the nineteenth

century,' Olly began solemnly. 'It's all the fault of my great-great grandfather, William Christie.'

Josh listened in amazement as Olly told him how William had removed the sacred scroll from the old tomb, and then made a translation of the curse.

'So, what happened next?' Josh asked. 'Did he die in some weird way?'

'No, *he* didn't die,' Olly replied. 'That wasn't the curse. His first-born son, Edmund, was the one who died – of tuberculosis in 1907. He was seventeen.'

'But that wasn't particularly strange back in those days,' Josh pointed out. 'People died of nasty diseases all the time.'

'I haven't finished,' Olly said. 'William had a second son called Francis. Well, William died in 1939, and while Francis and *his* son, Adam – his *first-born* son – were going through William's things, they found his diaries and the pot with the papyrus pages in it. The diaries showed that William forgot all about the curse till his son died. Then he began to wonder if it was the curse that had killed Edmund.'

Josh looked doubtfully at Olly. 'And you're not going to tell me that Adam died, too, are you?'

'You bet I am,' responded Olly. She was about to continue, when a strange booming sound interrupted her. It echoed within the tomb – coming from outside the room, from further up the passageway. Josh and Olly looked at one another, puzzled by the noise. It was a few moments before they realised that they were hearing the distorted sound of a human voice. Someone was shouting in alarm.

The voice drew closer, and a figure ran past the chamber they were in. Olly was shocked to realise that it was Jonathan. Wondering what could possibly have happened, she and Josh ran after him as he burst into the lower chamber where Professor Christie was working.

'What's all the noise?' the professor exclaimed. 'I can't hear myself think!'

'Professor! It's gone!' Jonathan Welles gasped.

The professor and the two friends stared at him.

'What's gone?' Professor Christie asked.

'The stone,' Jonathan cried. 'Someone has stolen the Elephantine Stone!'

Chapter Two

Thief!

Beyond fertile fields and across the wide waters of the Nile – some six kilometres from the remote, tomb-pocked Valley of the Kings – lies the town of Luxor. Two police officers came from there in response to Jonathan Welles' telephone call. Polite and efficient, they examined the trailer from which the Elephantine Stone had been stolen, making notes and asking questions in fluent English.

The small trailer seemed very crowded. Olly and Josh were there, along with the professor and Jonathan and Olly's gran, sixty-three-year-old Audrey Beckmann. She sat between the two youngsters, her sharp, intelligent eyes taking everything in. Her grey hair was cut into a short, smart bob. She wore a crisp white blouse, khaki trousers and neat suede boots.

There was an air of gloom in the trailer as Professor Christie explained to the police officers the importance of the lost stone. 'It is an artefact of immeasurable value,' he told them. 'Please do everything you can to find the thief and retrieve the stone.'

The officer in charge looked at a photograph that had been taken shortly after the Elephantine Stone's discovery. 'Artefacts such as this command very high prices,' he said. 'It is possible that the stone is already on its way to the illegal markets in Cairo.' He saw the look of despair on the professor's face. 'But do not fear, Professor Christie, we will ask many questions of many people. *Inshallah* – God willing – we will find the stone and return it to you.' The police officers stepped down from the trailer.

'I can't believe it,' Olly wailed. 'We were down in the tomb talking about robbers from thousands of years ago, and at the same time, someone was up here, making off with the Elephantine Stone!'

'At least we've still got photos, and copies of the

writings on the stone,' Josh pointed out. 'It's not like we all have to give up and go home.'

Jonathan frowned at him. 'That's not the point, Josh,' he sighed. Olly could understand his frustration – her father wasn't blaming Jonathan, but she knew he must feel responsible for the loss.

Professor Christie lifted his hand. 'No, Josh is right,' he said. 'We must continue our work and allow the police to do theirs.'

Audrey Beckmann stood up. 'There's obviously nothing more we can do,' she said. She looked at Josh and Olly. 'You two need to wash that dirt off your hands and come over to my trailer for your lessons.'

Olly looked up at her gran in surprise. 'I won't be able to concentrate on lessons with all this going on,' she said.

Audrey Beckmann frowned. 'Oh, I think I'll be able to help you concentrate,' she said. 'You know the rules, Olly – three hours of schooling a day during term-time.' She headed for the door. 'I'll expect to see the two of you in five minutes – with your Maths books.'

The door closed sharply behind her.

Olly looked appealingly at her father. 'Maybe we

could help look for the stone,' she said. 'I've been thinking, and . . .'

Professor Christie stared at her in alarm. 'No, Olivia,' he said firmly. 'We'll leave the investigation to the police.' He turned to Jonathan. 'We mustn't dwell on this,' he said. 'There's still plenty of work to be done. I've found some interesting inscriptions in the burial chamber – I'd like you to come and look at them with me. And bring the translation of the stone – I think it will be useful.'

Olly and Josh left the trailer.

Josh looked at his friend. 'So, *what* have you been thinking?' he asked.

'I've got a theory,' Olly said, her bright eyes gleaming. 'The thief must have kept watch on the trailer, and sneaked in the moment Jonathan's back was turned, right?' She looked at Josh. 'Which means it has to be someone who works here – maybe one of the diggers.'

Josh nodded. 'And *that* means the stone is probably still here,' he said excitedly. 'Hidden away till the end of the day.'

'Exactly,' Olly agreed. 'So as soon as Gran has finished with us, we're going to find the stone and unmask the thief!'

Josh grinned. 'Can you imagine the look on Jonathan's face when we hand the stone back to him? It'll be great!'

They stopped off to wash their grimy hands and to pick up their school books before heading over to Audrey Beckmann's trailer.

'So, what happened to Adam?' Josh asked curiously. Olly had interrupted the tale of her family curse to listen to Jonathan, and Josh was eager now to hear the end – in spite of all that had happened in between.

Olly stared at him, her mind still full of plans for finding the Elephantine Stone. 'Huh? Oh – Great-uncle Adam. Well, apparently, when he read about the curse, he got really jumpy – like you would if you believed in curses and you were the first-born son who was going to die! His father tried to convince him that the curse couldn't possibly be real, but Adam was totally spooked. He thought he could end the whole curse thing by taking the sacred papyrus text to Egypt, and putting it back in the tomb it came from.' Olly shook her head. 'Big mistake.'

'He died?' Josh asked.

'His ship was hit by a really big storm and sank

without trace,' Olly told him. 'Great-uncle Adam – and the pot and the sacred text and everything – went down with the ship.' She looked solemnly at Josh. 'The curse had claimed its second victim.'

Josh frowned. 'But Adam only died because he believed in the curse,' he said. 'Otherwise, he wouldn't have been on that ship in the first place. That's exactly how these curse things work. You tell someone they're cursed, and then the curse comes true – but only because they *believe* in it.'

Olly sighed. 'Uncle Douglas didn't believe in it – and it got him, too,' she said.

Josh stared. 'Who's Uncle Douglas?'

They had almost reached the trailer now. The door was opened from inside and Olly's gran appeared in the doorway. 'Come along, you two,' she called. 'You won't learn anything by mooching about out there.' She withdrew, leaving the door open for them.

'What about Uncle Douglas?' Josh hissed urgently to Olly.

'Later,' Olly whispered back. 'Don't mention him in front of Gran – she doesn't like it.'

* * *

It was late in the afternoon when Olly and Josh finally escaped the watchful eye of Audrey Beckmann, and Josh was eager to hear the rest of Olly's family history. 'So, how did your Uncle Douglas die?' he asked her.

'He was killed in a car crash in 1964,' she replied. 'He was nineteen. He was my dad's older brother – Grandad's first-born son. Dad was born next, then Aunt Anna.'

Josh was quiet for a few moments as he took this in. 'Why did you tell me not to mention him in front of your gran?' he asked at length. 'She's your *mother's* mother, isn't she? She wasn't directly related to your dead uncle. Why would it bother her?'

Olly shrugged. 'Gran just doesn't like anyone talking about the curse. We never mention it in front of her.'

'I get it,' Josh said. 'She thinks the curse is a load of rubbish?'

'That's what Dad says,' Olly responded. 'But if you ask me, I think it's the other way around. I think Gran's afraid that the curse is *real* – that's why she won't talk about it.'

Josh stared at her. The idea that Olly's level-headed gran might actually believe in the curse was the most alarming thing that he had heard so far. 'What does your dad think about all this?' he asked.

Olly frowned. 'It's difficult to tell,' she said. 'He makes out like it's all mumbo-jumbo, but the reason he got into archaeology in the first place was because of the curse. He did loads of research – following the curse back and checking it out in the archives and so on. And here's the thing – he found old inscriptions in the British Museum which said that copies of all the old sacred texts, from all the tombs, were kept in the Hall of Records.' She looked at her friend. 'So, you have to ask yourself – is Dad searching for the Talismans of the Moon because he wants to open the Hall of Records for academic purposes? Or is he doing it so that he can find a copy of the text that William Christie took from Hathtut's tomb, and put it back – like Great-uncle Adam was trying to do – and end the curse?'

'Wow!' breathed Josh. 'You weren't kidding when you said you had a weird family.'

Olly gave a faint smile. She didn't tell him the thing that sometimes kept her awake at night. The

curse only mentioned the death of first-born *sons* –
but what would happen if no boys were born? Her
Aunt Anna had no children, so Olly was the only
child in her entire family. Would the lack of boy
children break the curse – or might it switch to the
first-born daughter, instead?

The searing heat of the day had lessened, but
the canyon was still as hot as an oven as the two
friends walked over to where the diggers were
labouring. Olly looked out across the site. There
was no sign of Jonathan or her father. She assumed
they must be down in the tomb. The labourers
were being supervised by Mohammed, a handsome
young Egyptian who had been hired for his
knowledge of the valley and its history. He was a
student of Egyptology from Cairo University, and
he spoke fluent English. Olly liked him – he was
always polite and courteous, although he was quick
to bark orders at anyone who wasn't working hard
enough.

'So, where do we start our search for the stone?'
Josh asked. 'We can't exactly go through everyone's
pockets.'

Olly looked around thoughtfully. There was a
tent nearby where much-needed bottled drinking

water was kept. Many of the diggers kept small bundles of possessions there, too, heaped together out of the direct sunlight. 'If you kept watch for me,' Olly suggested, 'I could nip into that tent and have a quick look through the packs.'

Josh's forehead wrinkled. 'Are you sure that's a good idea?' he asked.

Olly frowned. 'Well, I wouldn't do it under normal circumstances,' she admitted. 'But we do want to find the Elephantine Stone, don't we?'

'We do.'

'And it's not like I'll be prying,' Olly continued, 'because I'll just feel the packs, and if I come across anything that feels like the stone, then I'll look properly. That's OK, isn't it?'

'I suppose so,' Josh agreed. He shrugged. 'Anyway, this is really important. OK. I'll keep watch – but be quick.'

Olly nodded, and with a final nervous glance at the workers, she turned and slipped into the tent.

To her dismay, she found Jonathan standing there, a bottle of water in his hand and a very unhappy look on his face. 'Get in here, Josh,' he ordered.

Josh slunk in and stood at Olly's side.

'I can't believe what I just heard,' Jonathan said. 'You can't just go through people's private possessions! What were you thinking?'

'We want to help find the stone,' Olly explained.

'You can help by keeping out of the way,' Jonathan told her firmly. His eyes moved from Olly to Josh and then back to Olly. 'No more bright ideas, OK?'

Olly nodded. 'OK,' she muttered.

Jonathan herded them out of the tent and went to speak to Mohammed, leaving Olly and Josh rather crestfallen.

'That was terrible,' Olly groaned. 'Maybe trying to find the stone isn't such a good idea after all.'

Josh shook his head. 'We can't give up yet,' he said. 'Listen, I have a plan. Why don't we go over to the canteen and have a word with Ahmed? He might know something.'

Olly's face brightened. 'That's an excellent plan,' she said. 'We could ask him a few casual questions about the diggers. He knows everything that goes on here. He'll be able to tell us if anyone has been acting suspiciously. Good one, Josh!'

* * *

The canteen was a large wooden shack over at the southern end of the site. It was run by Ahmed Farfour, a beefy, bald-headed man who acted as cook, waiter and source of all news, gossip and information for the entire valley. Ahmed had the radio on. It was playing traditional Saidi music, with its reedy swirls of notes and its strong, hypnotic rhythms.

It was quite normal for the two friends to go into the canteen via the back entrance. That way, they emerged behind the counter – amongst Ahmed's tempting foodstuffs. Olly was a particular fan of the thick, syrupy pastries, and the freshly-squeezed orange juice, sweetened with sugar-cane. Josh liked the new-baked pitta bread and the dipping sauces – hummus, babaganoush and spicy tahini.

The back door was ajar when they arrived. Olly stopped so suddenly that Josh almost walked into her. Before he could speak, Olly gestured to him to keep quiet.

Through the narrow crack in the door, Josh heard Ahmed's voice. He was speaking in heavily accented English. At first Josh thought he was talking to someone in the canteen, but after a moment he realised that Ahmed must be speaking on a mobile phone.

'I cannot get away yet,' Ahmed was saying, his voice an urgent, hushed growl. 'No, not today. It is impossible. Tell him I will meet him at the souk in Luxor – at the stall of Khaled the spice merchant. Yes, that's the place. Tell him to be there early – soon after dawn. And tell him that, if we can come to an agreement, it will prove profitable for us both. Speak of this to no one else.'

The two friends stared at one another. Josh gestured to Olly and they crept away from the building. 'What do you think he was talking about?' Olly asked. 'It sounded very suspicious to me.'

Josh nodded. 'I reckon Ahmed stole the Elephantine Stone,' he whispered. 'I'm sure he was arranging to hand it over to someone.'

'Amazing!' Olly breathed. 'Case solved. We have to tell Dad and Jonathan.'

She turned to go, but Josh caught her arm. 'I don't think that's such a great idea right now,' he hissed. 'Ahmed has probably hidden the stone. What if he convinces them that what we heard was totally innocent? They'll go mad – especially after what Jonathan just said.'

'You're right,' Olly said thoughtfully. Then suddenly, her eyes lit up. 'Which means we'll have to go to Luxor first thing tomorrow morning, hide near the spice merchant's stall and catch Ahmed, red-handed, selling the stone!'

Josh thought about this. There seemed to him to be a major flaw in Olly's plan. 'How are we going to get there?' he asked. 'It's six kilometres away on the other side of the river, and we can't exactly ask Jonathan or your dad to drive us over there at that time of day.'

Olly frowned. 'Good point,' she said. But then she smiled. 'Got it! You get on well with Abdullah, and *he* looks after the donkeys. Do you think you could persuade him to lend us a couple?'

'He'll want something in exchange,' Josh said. 'I'll have to think about what we could give him.' He glanced at Olly. 'You know, we'll need to get up pretty early to be in Luxor by dawn.'

Olly groaned. 'I'll never wake up in time.'

'Don't worry, I've got an alarm on my watch,' Josh told her, and grinned. 'I'll make sure you're awake.'

Olly frowned at him. 'Just wake me gently,' she said. 'Otherwise I'll be in a terrible mood all morning – and you won't like that at all.' And with that she turned and walked off to her trailer.

Josh gazed after her with a quiet smile, wondering what was going to be more dangerous – spying on Ahmed, or waking Olly up in the middle of the night.

Chapter Three

The Souk at Luxor

The Valley of the Kings was shrouded in darkness as Josh and Olly made their stealthy way towards the donkey pen at the far eastern end of the archaeological dig. Behind a wicker fence, the animals stood, quiet and still, in the grey gloom. Abdullah, the donkey-boy, lay sleeping in his hut, his head pillowed on two comic books that Josh had traded for the loan of two donkeys.

'Which are ours?' Olly whispered, leaning over the fence and patting the nearest donkey. It nuzzled her hand, sniffing for food. 'Sorry, donkey – I haven't got anything for you,' she murmured fondly.

'Abdullah said take any of them,' Josh replied.

A few minutes later, they led two donkeys out of the pen. It took Olly several attempts to mount up – the donkey kept moving every time she tried to climb on board. Josh sat astride his own docile animal, watching and grinning at her efforts.

'This is hard work,' Olly puffed, finally getting herself in place on the donkey's back. She pulled the reins and gave the donkey a tap both sides with her heels. 'C'mon, boy,' she said. 'Let's go!' The donkey didn't move.

Josh made a clicking noise with his tongue and gently twitched the reins. His own donkey responded immediately, trotting obediently forwards along the track.

'Hey! Wait for me,' Olly called. 'I can't get mine started!' She leant close to the donkey's long velvet ears. 'Listen, boy,' she said. 'We're on a vital mission here, so could you please get going? I'll bring you an apple when we get back. Is that a deal?'

The donkey lowered its shaggy head and sniffed the ground, as if hoping to find some grass. It didn't move so much as a single hoof.

Olly watched as Josh guided his own donkey back up the path. Without speaking, he caught hold of her reins. He made a small chirruping sound, and the two donkeys began to walk along, side by side.

'What are you?' Olly asked with a chuckle. 'Josh the donkey-whisperer, or something?'

Josh laughed. 'They trust me,' he told her. 'Animals are smart like that. What can I say?'

Olly smiled, then yawned. 'Whose idea was it to get up so early anyway?' she groaned.

'Yours,' Josh reminded her. He clicked his tongue and the two donkeys broke into a gentle trot.

A thousand stars filled the sky above, their sharp glitter beginning to fade as the first hint of dawn crept out of the east. The jagged cliffs cast long, forbidding shadows, and as the donkeys trotted down the road, Olly noticed the entrances to the old tombs gaping like black mouths in the hillsides.

Sixty-three tombs had been found in the Valley – sixty-three tombs for sixty-three dead pharaohs, Olly thought. She glanced over her shoulder and shivered. In the pre-dawn gloom and silence of the canyon, it was almost possible to believe that wicked, age-old eyes were watching their progress from those dark holes in the cliffs. She was glad when, a few minutes later, they left the mountains behind and began the descent through the lush green fields that surrounded the town of New Gurna.

It took them about half an hour to reach the Baladi ferry dock. By then, the eastern sky was filling with light. While Josh paid the ferryman, Olly looked back again. The phantoms of the Valley had been banished by the dawn, and the cliffs glowed golden in the clear light.

The water rippled under the ferry as it crossed the great river. The trip across the Nile took only a few minutes, and soon the ferry docked on the east bank and the few early passengers disembarked. Olly and Josh paid a boy to look after their donkeys; from here they would walk.

They skirted the ruins of Luxor Temple with its massive, towering walls and impressive granite statues of Ramses II. From there they made their way along the Sharia Cleopatra to the Midan al-Mahatta. The souk was already beginning to bustle. The market was a maze of canvas-covered stalls, selling a huge variety of goods – hand-woven rugs, jewellery, brass and copperware, appliqué wall-hangings, leather, perfumes, exotic musical instruments. And, seemingly at every step they took, there was a smiling street-hawker or a vendor calling out to them to buy.

'*La! La! Imshi!*' Josh said to a particularly persistent boy who was clawing at his clothes and begging for money. 'No! No! Go away!'

'Keep on the lookout for a stall that sells spices,' Olly reminded him.

They made their way slowly through the narrow alleys. All around them were men in the loose-fitting galabia robes, old women in black with covered heads, and younger women in long gowns of brightly-coloured cotton.

The hubbub of the bartering and talking and shouting was so loud that the two friends could hardly hear themselves think. And that wasn't their only problem. They soon came to a long, winding alley, filled with the sights and scents of a hundred different spices, herbs and dyes. They lay in heaped pyramids – warm yellow saffron, fiery red paprika and glowing ochre curries. Baskets were stuffed with dates and figs and nuts, oranges and limes and pomegranates. Then there were juicy tomatoes, fragrant bunches of aromatic coriander and mint, piles of green peppers, onions and garlic bulbs and huge tubs filled with rice.

Josh looked at Olly. 'Which stall belongs to Khaled, do you think?'

Olly blinked at the bewildering scene in front of her. 'I don't have a clue,' she said helplessly. 'Now what shall we do?'

'Maybe we should just ask?' Josh suggested.

'No.' Olly shook her head. 'We need to keep out of sight. Ahmed could turn up at any minute.'

'What if we split up?' Josh said. 'You can hide at this end of the row – and I'll go and hide at the other. Ahmed will have to come past one of us – then we can keep tabs on him till he does the deal.'

Olly nodded. 'Good plan,' she agreed. She looked around. An old stall-holder in dark blue robes was seated among heaps of oranges and bananas and tomatoes. Behind him, wicker baskets were stacked high. Olly walked down alongside the stall, then slipped behind the stacks of baskets and disappeared from sight. Through the lattice of wickerwork, she watched as Josh made his way quickly along the winding corridor of stalls, and vanished.

Olly kept quite still, breathing in the bewildering mix of exotic scents and studying the dark faces of the stall-holders, wondering which one might be Khaled.

Minutes passed. More people came into the souk. Voices were raised, haggling over prices – the sellers asking too much, the buyers offering too little – in the age-old way of Egyptian culture. She found the whole thing fascinating and was quite surprised when she glanced at her watch and realised she had been waiting for fifteen minutes already.

Hunger pangs reminded her that they had set off on this trip without bringing anything to eat. Bananas were piled temptingly within arm's-reach of the baskets. A banana or two would make a pleasant snack, Olly thought. She felt in her pockets and drew out some Egyptian money, then reached cautiously through the barrier of baskets and helped herself to a couple of bananas, carefully placing the money on top of the remaining pile.

She had eaten the first banana and was peeling the second, when she saw Ahmed. Her heart jumped. He walked along the row of stalls and stopped at the one right next to her hiding place.

Olly hardly dared breathe as she watched him. He spoke to the stall-holder – calling him Khaled!

She grinned – she was in exactly the right place to see and hear everything. She kept as quiet and still as she could and watched Ahmed chatting with Khaled – apparently just passing the time of day.

A couple of minutes had gone by, when a tall thin man in a T-shirt and faded jeans approached the stall. He was much darker than the locals – Olly guessed he was Ethiopian or Somalian.

Ahmed greeted him with a handshake. 'Are you Ghedi?' he asked, speaking in English. The man nodded. 'Good,' Ahmed said. 'I have been waiting for you.'

Olly assumed that this new man either didn't speak Arabic, or spoke in a dialect that Ahmed didn't understand – English was often used as an intermediary language.

Ahmed led the man between the stalls. Olly backed stealthily away as they approached her hiding place. She squeezed herself into a narrow space between rough wooden trestles, edging deeper into cover, anxious not to ruin everything by being seen. A tap on the shoulder made her jump and whirl round. It was Josh.

Her heart pounding, Olly put her finger to her lips and gestured towards the two men. Josh nodded and they listened in silence. Ahmed and the other man were conversing in low voices, but the friends could just about hear what was being said.

'You have no work permit?' Ahmed asked.

Ghedi shook his head.

'I can help you, I believe,' Ahmed told him. 'The English will not normally hire anyone without the correct papers, but I can tell them you are a relation of mine and give you a job in the canteen. The pay is not high, and you will need to reimburse me for my efforts on your behalf. You will give me twenty-five percent of your wages – is that understood?'

Ghedi nodded. Ahmed smiled and took his hand. 'Then we have a deal – and I have a new assistant,' he said. 'Come – if anyone asks, you are my distant cousin from Abu Simbel. You will work hard, but the food is free.' The two men laughed and Ahmed led Ghedi away.

Olly turned to Josh. 'He was only hiring someone without a work permit,' she groaned. 'What a let-down!'

Josh's face showed his disappointment. 'I suppose we'd better get back to camp,' he sighed. 'If we're gone too long, we'll be in trouble.'

But before they could move, trouble hit them right where they were.

Without any warming, the trestles behind which they were hiding were suddenly pulled away. An angry face appeared – the old stall-holder had spotted them. He pointed to the half-peeled banana in Olly's hand. '*Harami!*' he shouted, reaching down to grab them. '*El-ha'ni! Harami!*'

Olly recognised the words: *Thief! Help – thief!*

'No! We're not thieves!' Olly yelled, squirming away from his grasping fingers. 'I left some money – honestly, I did!'

But the stall-holder clearly didn't understand English – and he was very angry. He was shouting now, calling out names: 'Essam! Bashir!'

The two friends backed away from the old man, only to find that two large, younger men had appeared behind them.

'Run!' Olly yelled. She bobbed under the grasping arms of one of the men and dived to one side. Josh was only a second behind her, slipping past the other man, just out of reach. People were stopping and staring now. Essam and Bashir were shouting as they pursued the escaping friends.

'I paid for the bananas!' Olly yelled. But the

continued shouts of her pursuers made it clear her words had not been understood.

The two friends ran, ducking and weaving between people, threading their way along the crowded alley, gasping for breath as they ran, helter-skelter, away from the pursuing men. They jumped over hillocks of fruit and vegetables and pounded through stalls draped with colourful robes and embroidered rugs and tapestries. They were trying to find a way out of the souk, but they soon got hopelessly lost in the maze of tangled alleyways. Every street seemed blocked by crowds, and in every direction there were more stalls and more people.

They pelted along a narrow street. There were stalls on one side and sand-coloured single-storey shops on the other. Josh pointed towards a small side street.

'Yes!' Olly gasped – desperate to get out of the labyrinth of the souk. They plunged headlong down the side street. On one side there was a doorway, screened by a striped awning. Josh grabbed Olly by the arm and dived through the entrance.

The friends came to a halt and looked around.

They were in a large, dark store-room of some kind. Carpets and baskets of all shapes and sizes were stacked in profusion, alongside huge pottery urns, carved furniture and gleaming brass ornaments. Josh dragged Olly down behind a large wooden chest. Trying not to pant too loudly, the friends listened out for their pursuers. Soon they heard familiar loud, angry voices outside the front of the building.

It was Essam and Bashir – still close on their trail.

'We can't keep running,' Josh whispered. 'We have to hide.' He pointed to some carpet rolls that were heaped nearby. 'I know,' he said, jumping up and quickly unrolling one of the carpets. 'Lie on this!'

Olly stared at him in confusion. 'What?'

'Just do it!' Josh panted. 'Trust me. Mum did it once in a movie.' He pointed to a large papyrus basket with a lid. 'I'll hide in there,' he said. 'Now, hurry up!'

With deep misgivings, Olly lay down on the carpet. Josh grasped the edge of the rug and pulled it up over her. Olly felt Josh heave at the carpet and then she was being rolled over and over in complete darkness.

She came to a stop face up – fortunately – but totally trapped by the weight of the carpet. Her arms were pinned to her sides and the heavy material pressed against her face, filling her nose with the smell of new-woven wool. She couldn't move – she could only just breathe!

She heard Josh's voice coming from one end of the carpet roll. 'Are you OK?' he hissed.

'Just about,' Olly gasped. 'Hide yourself!'

She lay in the suffocating silence for a few moments, hoping that Josh would have time to get under cover. She twisted her head to get her mouth into a position where she could breathe more easily, and saw a small patch of light about a metre above her – the end of the roll. Then she heard voices and the sound of footsteps. Their pursuers had entered the room.

As Olly lay there, listening to Essam and Bashir's angry voices, she realised that she was now completely helpless – without Josh's assistance she could be stuck in the carpet for ever!

Chapter Four

The Plot

Once Josh was sure that Olly was safely out of sight in the rolled-up carpet, he ran for the big papyrus basket, yanked the lid off and jumped inside. He fitted the lid back in place, trying to breathe quietly and hoping that his heart was not beating as loudly as it sounded to his own ears.

Moments after he had secured the lid, he heard Essam and Bashir enter the room, speaking rapidly in Arabic. He could hear other voices too. Josh guessed that they must belong to the owners of the shop. The conversation rose and fell for some time. Josh didn't know much Arabic, and he had no idea what was being said, although he could guess that the main subject must be the two young vagabonds who had absconded from the old man's stall.

Eventually the voices moved away. It sounded as if Bashir and Essam had been convinced that there were no thieves hiding inside. Josh let out a quiet sigh of relief. He was about to climb out of the basket when he heard new voices approaching. He ducked down again, groaning inwardly and hoping that these newcomers would pass by.

He was out of luck. The voices got louder – two men, speaking in English, entered the room. Josh could hear that one had an Arabic accent, but the other sounded like an American.

'We can speak freely here,' said the Arab. 'The owner is a friend of mine – he will say nothing.'

'Will he want *baksheesh* – a cut of the money?' the American demanded, his voice low and suspicious.

'A small token, that is all,' replied the Arab. 'A trifle. Once our friend in Cairo pays us what he has promised, there will be enough to satisfy everyone.'

'Do you have the stone with you?' the American asked.

'No,' responded the Arab. 'But it is safe.'

The American's voice grew harsh. 'What do you mean? Where is it?'

'Have no fear, my friend,' the Arab said quickly. 'I have hidden it away – in the last place they would think to look – in the tomb of Setiankhra.'

Josh held his breath, his mind reeling from what he was hearing. The two men were discussing the Elephantine Stone!

'Are you crazy?' the American snarled. 'That place is crawling with people.'

'I'll get it for you after nightfall – when the tomb is deserted,' said the Arab. 'I'll bring it to you then.'

'No!' snapped the American. 'That's too late. My orders are to hand it over in Cairo this evening. You fool – why didn't you bring it with you?'

'It was too dangerous.'

The American's voice came again, quiet but savage. 'I gave my word that he'd have the stone today,' he growled. 'He doesn't accept excuses. If I let him down, bad things will happen to me.' His voice became deadly. 'And if bad things happen to *me*, I'll make sure bad things happen to *you*. Understand?'

'Between noon and two in the afternoon, the tomb will be empty,' the Arab gasped. He sounded half-choked – as though the American had a stranglehold on him. 'The diggers rest then. I'll get the stone for you.'

'No. I'll come for it myself,' the American growled. 'I don't trust you to do this right.'

'But you won't be allowed into the tomb,' protested the Arab. 'The professor is very cautious – especially since the theft.'

'Let me worry about that,' replied the American. 'I'll be waiting for you in the tomb at midday. You just make sure you're there with the stone. Got that?'

The Arab gave a gasp – Josh assumed he had been released by the brutal American. 'I'll be there.' He lowered his voice. 'Do you have the money?'

'You'll get your share,' said the American. 'Now, get lost!'

Muttering a few final words, the Arab left. Josh listened intently, waiting in cramped silence for the American to leave too. But the man seemed in no hurry. Josh could hear subdued movements – the rustle of cellophane, the faint snap of a cigarette lighter. Then a weight came down on the basket and Josh was squashed into an even smaller space. The American was clearly sitting on Josh's hiding place!

Josh could smell cigarette smoke and hear the man muttering to himself, but he couldn't make out what the man was saying. He bit his lip, his neck aching from the unnatural position he was in. But the agony didn't last long. The American stood up and Josh heard his footsteps moving away.

Josh heaved the lid off his basket and tumbled out. He rubbed his aching legs, crouching on hands and knees as the numbness in his feet gave way to maddening pins and needles. He tried to stand up, but his deadened feet wouldn't obey, so he crawled over to the pile of rolled carpets. 'Olly?' he whispered loudly. 'Are you OK?'

'Not really!' came a muffled reply. 'Get me out of here!'

Josh got up on to his knees and grasped the edge of the carpet. Then new voices made him turn in alarm. Someone was approaching and there wasn't time for him to reach the basket. He tried to scramble to his feet, but fell. In desperation, he crawled up the pile of carpets and burrowed down between two of them. He had only just got himself out of sight when he heard cheerful Arabic voices enter the room.

Someone barked orders and Josh felt the heap

of rolled carpets shift under him. He lifted his head and peeped out.

Two men were walking out of the room carrying a carpet between them. Josh had to stifle a groan of dismay – the men were carrying off the carpet in which Olly was still hiding!

Quickly, Josh eased himself out of his hiding place and scrambled down the pile of carpets. He ran to the doorway – his feet were working now, although they buzzed and stung as though swarming with wasps – and peered outside. At the end of the narrow side street, he could see a waiting truck. The carpet had been loaded on to the back, along with some furniture and ornaments. Josh stared in horror as he heard the truck's engine splutter to life.

Ignoring the tingling in his feet, Josh ran faster than he had ever run in his life. The truck was just pulling away as he made a flying leap for the backboard. His feet dragged for a few seconds as he struggled to pull himself on board, but with a final supreme effort, he managed to haul himself up over the backboard and fall, sprawling, into the back of the truck.

It took him a few minutes to get his breath back.

Then he crawled over to Olly's carpet and pulled one end open. 'Are you OK?' he called.

'No!' came the muffled reply. 'What's going on?'

'We're in the back of a truck.'

'I worked that out for myself!' replied Olly's exasperated voice. 'Unroll me!'

Josh tried to unwrap the carpet, but it was wedged between two heavy pieces of furniture. He put his mouth to the end again. 'I can't. Can you wriggle out?' he asked.

'No!'

He reached into the roll and felt Olly's hair under his fingers. He decided that trying to drag her out by her hair wasn't a good idea – but maybe the other end?

The truck was picking up speed now, bouncing and jolting over the uneven roads as it headed south, out of the town. Josh clambered down to the other end of the carpet and reached up inside. He felt a shoe.

'Olly?' he called into the roll. 'I'm going to pull. You try and help me.' He got a firm grip on the shoe. 'On the count of three,' Josh shouted. 'One – two – three!' He pulled with all his strength – and nearly fell off the back of the truck as the shoe suddenly came away in his hand!

Defeated, he went back to the head of the carpet. 'Olly? You'll have to stay where you are till the truck stops,' he called. 'Sorry.'

'I'll give *you* sorry when I get out of here!' came the muted response.

Josh did his best to make himself comfortable. They had left the town behind now and the truck was moving rapidly along an open road. He had the horrible feeling that this might take a while!

Josh was right. It was half an hour before they came to a small village. The truck pulled off the main road and began to negotiate small side streets. Eventually, it pulled up outside a large, two-storey house and the driver and his assistant got out and went to the front door.

Josh slipped quietly over the side of the truck and watched from behind a low wall. The front door swung upon, there was a brief conversation, and then the backboard of the van was lowered and Olly's carpet was carried, shoulder-high, into the house.

* * *

Olly could guess what was going on. She felt herself tipping at an odd angle and then the carpet roll jack-knifed, folding her up with it. But the change helped. She was finally able to free her arms from their confined position at her sides. She dragged them up across her chest and fought to stretch them out above her head. She had just managed this exhausting feat when the carpet straightened out again, and she was sent crashing to the floor with a jolt that knocked all the wind out of her.

Olly listened for a few moments and heard voices receding. She gave a sigh of relief – she'd been worried that they might unroll the carpet right then and there. But it seemed they were happy to leave it rolled up for the time being. She waited a few moments – no voices, so hopefully, no people. She squirmed on to her front and began to wriggle slowly along the roll.

Now that her arms were up above her head, it was far easier for Olly to move. It only took her half a minute to get out. She wiped the fluff and sweat off her face, delighted to be free at last. 'Phew!' she breathed, feeling slightly dizzy. 'Josh goes in the carpet next time!'

She hobbled awkwardly across the room in her

remaining shoe – then decided it would be easier to go barefoot and kicked it off. The other, she assumed, was still on the truck where Josh had removed it.

She was in a bedroom. Olly could see that it must belong to a wealthy woman, for the bed was draped with colourful silks, the dressing-table littered with perfumes and cosmetics. She crept to the open door, keeping herself out of sight and listening intently. It didn't sound as if there was anyone nearby. It was time to make her escape from the house. She eased the door open, and very nearly let out a howl of shock as she came face to face with Josh!

Hurriedly, he pushed her back into the bedroom. 'We can't get out that way,' he whispered fiercely. 'They're coming. I only just slipped past.'

'You should have stayed outside,' Olly told him.

'I thought you needed rescuing,' Josh replied.

Olly grinned. 'Thanks, but I managed to rescue myself.' She sighed. 'And now we *both* need rescuing.'

A quick glance round the room soon told her that the window was the only other possible exit. She padded across the floor and flung it open.

'There's a trellis,' she said softly. 'We can climb down.'

Josh tiptoed over. A thick-limbed old fig vine climbed the trellis, making it easy enough for the friends to scramble down. Josh clambered over the window sill. Olly followed.

'What about your shoe?' Josh asked, looking up and noticing Olly's bare feet above him.

'One shoe's not much use,' she replied. 'You lost the other one.'

'No. I've got it in my pocket,' Josh said.

Olly rolled her eyes. 'Now you tell me.' She edged back up the vine.

'Olly – no!' gasped Josh, but he knew it wouldn't make any difference.

Olly clambered in through the window, ran across the room and scooped up her shoe. As she was turning to leave, a group of people came in. They looked like a family – husband, wife and two young daughters – and they stared at her in surprise.

Olly waved her shoe at them. 'I just came by for this,' she explained. 'It's a really lovely carpet – I hope you enjoy it more than I did,' she added, as she raced back to the window.

The man stared at her, then began to speak in rapid Arabic.

Olly didn't stay to listen. She slipped lithely over the sill and came down the vine like a monkey.

Four astonished faces stared from the window above as the two friends sprinted along the road and disappeared around a corner.

'Well, that wasn't exactly how I expected things to go this morning,' Olly gasped. 'But at least we'll be able to catch that American when he turns up to get the stone.' She grinned. 'I think we did really well, all things considered!'

Josh looked at her. 'We still have to get back to the dig before midday, or it'll be too late,' he pointed out.

Olly nodded. She looked round. 'Where exactly are we?' she asked.

Josh frowned. 'The middle of nowhere,' he replied, and pointed. 'Luxor is off in that direction. How are we going to get back in time?'

Olly gave him a determined look. 'Maybe we can hitch a ride,' she said. 'Come on – we've got to make tracks if we're going to stop those thieves from getting away with the Elephantine Stone!'

Chapter Five

Danger From the Past

The sun shone down fiercely from high in the clear blue sky, making the road shimmer in the heat. The Nile lay to the left, silver and sparkling, and a rugged, stony emptiness stretched away to the right for as far as the eye could see. Flies buzzed and the wheels of the cart rumbled on the road as the donkey trotted steadily along.

Olly sat, perched among hessian sacks of beans, chatting away amiably in English to the uncomprehending driver, who gazed out between the donkey's long ears at the endless road ahead.

Josh was nested further back in the cart, lying back on the sacks, squinting in the dazzling light. 'You do realise he can't understand a single word you're saying, don't you?' Josh pointed out.

'I'm sure he recognises that I'm being friendly,' Olly replied. 'That's what counts.' She looked back. 'What's the time?'

Josh glanced at his watch. 'It's almost half-past ten.'

Olly frowned. They had been on the cart for half the morning, and there was still no sign of Luxor. The driver, a small, wizened man with only two teeth in his wide smile, had been happy to give them a lift. But Olly had been unable to explain, in her broken Arabic, that they were in a desperate hurry and had to get back to the Valley of the Kings by midday at the latest.

She decided to try again. 'Excuse me.'

The driver looked round at her and let out a laughing stream of Arabic – he seemed to find Olly very amusing.

'I'm glad I'm so entertaining,' she said patiently. 'But is there any way your lovely donkey could be persuaded to go just a little bit faster?'

The driver chuckled and nodded, but nothing happened.

'That's it,' Olly said, throwing her arms in the air. 'I give up.'

'The donkey's probably doing its best,' Josh said. 'How would *you* like to be hauling us around in this heat?'

'You're right,' Olly agreed. 'But it drives me crazy when cars and lorries go flying past, leaving us in a cloud of dust. I feel like I've been on this road *for ever*.' She turned and gazed ruefully at the winding road.

Josh squirmed about on the sacks, trying to get more comfortable. The donkey trotted on. Time trickled by.

It was a few minutes before noon when they finally got back to the ferry dock. The boy was still there with their donkeys. They had told him they would only be an hour, and he was angry at having been stuck there all morning, so they apologised profusely and gave him all the money they still had in their pockets. He counted it carefully, then broke into a wide smile and ran off, leaving them with the donkeys.

The ferry was crowded with tourists now. It was coming to the hottest part of the day, and most of the locals were resting in the shade.

Before long, Olly and Josh were across the river and riding back to camp on their donkeys. They were both relieved when they rode up through New Gurna and finally saw the mountain ridges of the Valley of the Kings looming ahead of them.

They dropped the donkeys off with Abdullah and ran towards the trailers. Olly noticed a few diggers sitting in the shade, resting. A trailer door opened as they approached and Olly's gran stepped down, her head shaded by a wide-brimmed straw hat. Olly could sense trouble ahead.

'I want a word with you two!' her gran said sternly. 'We were worried sick until Abdullah told us you'd borrowed two donkeys for a trip to Luxor. What on earth have you been up to?'

'I'm sorry, Gran,' Olly said, breathlessly. 'There's no time to explain. Where's Dad? It's really, really important.'

'Your father has driven down to the other end of the valley to do some research in another tomb,' her gran replied.

'What about Jonathan?' Josh asked.

'He's working in the office trailer,' Mrs Beckmann said. 'But I wouldn't disturb him if I were you – you're not exactly flavour of the month right now.'

'Can't help that, Gran,' Olly put in. 'We've got

vital information.' She and Josh ran over to the trailer that had been set up as the site office. Audrey Beckmann followed.

Olly was first through the trailer door, closely followed by Josh. They burst in to find Jonathan frowning over calculations on his laptop. The screen showed a 3D plan of Setiankhra's tomb as excavated so far.

Jonathan glared at them. 'You guys are in so much trouble,' he growled, as Audrey Beckmann appeared in the doorway behind them.

'But we know where the stone is!' Josh blurted.

'So that's it!' Mrs Beckmann said. 'I might have known.'

Jonathan stared at the friends. 'What are you talking about?' he demanded, his face grim. 'I told you two to stop all this nonsense.'

'Yes, but we've found out that the stone has been here all along!' Olly explained. 'It was stashed in Setiankhra's tomb. And an American man is coming here today – right now – to get it and take it to a buyer in Cairo! If we don't do something quickly, the stone will be gone for good!'

Jonathan stared at her. 'An American?' he repeated. 'Did you say an American?'

'Yes!' Olly and Josh exclaimed together.

'An American newspaper reporter was here just a few minutes ago,' Jonathan said. He looked at Audrey Beckmann. 'He told me he wanted to write a big piece on the tomb. He asked if he could take a look around.' His eyes widened in shocked realisation. 'He's in there right now!'

'I'll call the police,' Olly's gran said, moving to the desk and picking up the telephone.

Olly shook her head. 'They won't get here in time,' she pointed out. 'We have to stop him *now*!'

'She's right,' Jonathan said, jumping up and running for the door. 'I'll make sure he doesn't get away!'

Olly glanced at her gran and saw that she was completely immersed in her telephone call. Grabbing Josh by the arm, Olly dived for the door.

'Come on,' she said in a fierce whisper. 'Jonathan might need help!'

Josh didn't need any encouragement. Together, they jumped down from the trailer and raced towards the tomb entrance.

Jonathan had already disappeared inside by the time Olly and Josh arrived.

Josh caught hold of Olly and brought her to a

skidding halt at the entrance. 'We won't help by rushing in,' he said. 'Keep quiet and we'll find out what's going on first.'

Olly nodded and they crept silently through the entrance. A few metres down the first passageway, the electric lights began. Olly peered down the rest of the corridor, but it sloped at such an acute angle that she couldn't see the level area before the second drop.

Angry voices drifted up to her from the depths of the tomb. Olly swallowed nervously and looked at Josh. His face showed the same unease.

'That is a priceless artefact,' they heard Jonathan say. 'I can't let you take it.'

The American's reply was savage. 'Get out of my way!' There was the sound of a scuffle.

Olly and Josh ran down the sloping corridor. An alarming sight met their eyes. Jonathan and the American were locked together in a wild struggle, staggering to and fro across the floor of the chamber.

The American was a big man, taller and heavier than Jonathan and several years older. He was wearing jeans and a brown T-shirt. He had close-cut black hair and wild, dark eyes. Behind him,

Olly could see a third figure – small and slight – who she recognised instantly. His name was Habbib, and he was one of the oldest of the hired diggers. His face was tanned and wrinkled by the sun, his hair thin and grey. He clutched a bundle of cloth in his hands and Olly guessed immediately that it was wrapped around the Elephantine Stone.

Jonathan caught sight of Olly and his brother. 'Get out of here!' he shouted.

The American was quick to take advantage of his opponent's distraction. He delivered a crushing blow to the back of Jonathan's neck, which sent the younger man crashing to the floor. A vicious kick then threw Jonathan on to his side and sent him sliding a metre or so further down the slope, where he lay gasping and winded. The American took a step towards him.

'You leave him alone!' Olly shouted, too concerned for Jonathan's safety to care about drawing the thug's attention. The American turned towards her, his eyes glinting with menace.

'You're not getting past us!' Josh shouted, his voice shaking but determined.

A cruel grin spread over the American's face.

He obviously didn't think Olly and Josh posed much of an obstacle.

Olly acted almost without thinking. The American was standing on the level area between the two sloping corridors. Close to his feet was one of the wedges that had been pushed between the booby-trap stones. Olly sprang forwards and aimed a wild kick at the wedge. Her foot struck it hard, sending it skidding across the stones. With a yell of triumph, Olly threw herself backwards to safety.

Panting, she stared at the American, expecting the stones to tip at any moment and send him tumbling into darkness. But nothing happened. Olly's desperate gamble had failed. The ancient system of booby-traps no longer worked.

'The stone!' the American snarled, shooting a quick look over his shoulder at the terrified digger. 'Give it to me!' He reached out, his feet planted firmly on the ground, his eyes on Olly and Josh.

The digger stared at him but did not move. Olly could tell from the fear in his eyes that he had not been expecting violence.

'Give me the stone!' the American shouted. Shaking, the digger crept forwards and pushed the bundle into the American's hands. He glanced with troubled eyes at Olly and Josh, then backed away again.

The American clutched the bundle of cloth to his chest. His face became grim as he took a step towards the two friends. Olly and Josh stood side by side – blocking the corridor. Olly was scared, but determined. She wasn't going to let the man get past without a fight – even if the odds were hopeless.

The American's foot came down on a stone that shifted slightly under him. He lost his balance and fell to the floor. At the same moment, Olly heard an eerie, rushing, hissing sound coming from the walls, accompanied by an ominous grinding noise. Seconds later, a dozen or more stone spears shot from the pock-marked wall and flew across the corridor. They struck the far side, cracking and splintering to fragments. Surprised and startled, Olly threw herself to the floor, her arms coming up to shield her face from the flying shrapnel.

The American stared up in shock – if he had not fallen, the spikes would have impaled him! He staggered to his feet, his face distorted with anger as he stared down at Olly. But before he could make a move towards her, the air was filled with a wild blast of fine sand. He threw his hands up to protect his face, and staggered backwards, blinded and disorientated.

Olly heard the Egyptian let out a frantic stream of Arabic. She peered between her fingers and saw him cowering back from the ancient booby-trap. She could see where the sand was coming from – it came gushing out of the holes in the walls, cascading into the corridor like water from a burst pipe. But that was not all – blocks of stone began to rain down from the roof, thudding and crashing to the floor with deadly force.

The booby-traps had come alive – and they were far more lethal than Olly had ever imagined!

Chapter Six

The Tattoo

Olly stared at the mayhem she had created. It had never occurred to her that removing the wooden wedge would cause such chaos. As the booby-traps activated around her she scrambled to her feet, deafened by the noise and shaking with fear. She and Josh were already ankle-deep in the fine, spreading sand. Some of the falling stones were hitting the floor and crashing straight through – their weight dislodging the slabs that held the floor together. Sand poured through the gaps. More stones fell away.

Through the storm of fine sand, she saw Jonathan stagger to his feet and stumble towards the American, who was poised on the edge of the widening pit.

More gaps opened up in the floor with the roar and rumble of moving stone. A wide trench appeared in front of Olly. She jumped backwards just in time, pulling Josh with her as the ground under his feet also gave way.

The stones and sand were tumbling into a deep dark pit. The American was still on his feet, but he was at the heart of the area protected by the booby-traps, and the flood of sand held him fast. As Olly watched, the ground disappeared beneath him and he stumbled and fell in a sucking avalanche of sand. The wrapped bundle tumbled from his hands and thudded to the ground a metre away from the chasm.

Jonathan sprang forwards and grabbed hold of the American's hand. The weight of the falling man pulled him to the very brink of the gaping pit. But by lying flat on what remained of the floor, Jonathan was able to keep hold of the American and save him from plunging into the chasm.

Far below, faintly lit by the electric light, Olly could see the bottom of the pit. Among the sand and the fallen stones, row upon row of sharpened stone spikes pointed upwards – a deadly trap that had been waiting over three thousand years to claim its first victim.

Jonathan snatched hold of the American's other hand and slowly hauled him up, until he was able to catch hold of the stone lip of the pit. Relieved of the man's full weight, Jonathan was able to get to his knees, reach down and drag him back up to ground level.

Olly could see that there was no fight left in the man. He crawled to the side of the corridor and sat with his back to the wall, breathing heavily and nursing his shoulder.

A strange quiet descended on the tomb. The torrent of sand had lessened until it was no more than a trickle from the holes in the wall. The roof was pocked with gaps left by the fallen stones, and the entire level area between the sloping corridors of the tomb was gone. Instead a gaping pit yawned, threatening to swallow up intruders.

The terrified digger was crouched against the wall, some way down the lower corridor, staring up towards the booby-traps with frightened eyes and muttering anxiously under his breath.

Jonathan stood up and stared across the pit to where Olly was standing in stunned silence. 'Olly,' he said, wiping an arm across his sweating forehead. 'You are something else!'

'I didn't realise all this would happen!' she gasped. 'I just thought a stone would give way underneath him. Are you OK?'

'I'm fine.' He looked around the remains of the corridor. 'This place will never be the same again, though.' He shook his head. 'I can't work out whether you were incredibly brave or just plain crazy!'

Olly bit her lip – he had a point! But before she could think of a response, they all heard the sound of people approaching from the entrance.

Audrey Beckmann and Mohammed appeared at the head of a group of diggers. 'The police are on their way,' Mrs Beckmann said, staring at the debris. 'What on earth happened down here?'

Olly blinked at her. 'I set the booby-traps off, Gran,' she said quietly. 'And they were a bit more spectacular than I'd expected.'

Josh looked at his friend. 'What am I always telling you about not touching things?' he said, grinning.

Jonathan picked up the bundle of cloth from the floor and unwrapped it to reveal the Elephantine

Stone – still intact. He let out a sigh of relief, holding it up for them all to see. 'I think we'll let Olly get away with it this time,' he said with a laugh. 'What do you think?'

Half an hour had passed. Habbib and the subdued American were sitting on the ground with their backs to the office trailer, watched over by Mohammed the foreman and a couple of burly diggers. Habbib had his knees drawn up and his head in his hands. He was muttering constantly to himself – obviously traumatised by the events that had taken place in the tomb of Setiankhra. Documents in the American's wallet showed him to be going under the name of Benjamin Carter. He was sullen and withdrawn, offering no further information about himself and refusing offers of food and water.

Professor Christie had been contacted and was on his way back to the site from his researches in the tomb of Ramses II. The police were expected at any moment.

Jonathan had led a party of diggers into the tomb to start clearing up the mess. Some kind of bridge would need to be constructed to span the chasm that the booby-traps had created.

Olly and Josh were sitting with Audrey Beckmann in her trailer. Olly had the Elephantine Stone in her lap. She stroked it lightly with her fingertips. 'I knew we'd find it,' she said happily.

'You weren't supposed to be looking for it!' her gran said, glancing sternly from Olly to Josh. 'Do you have any idea of the damage you could have done to yourselves?'

Olly looked at her. 'Dad won't be mad, will he?' she asked. 'After all, we did get the stone back for him.'

Her gran's eyes glinted. 'It's not your father you need to worry about,' she said. 'It's me!'

Olly gave her a weak smile. 'Oh.'

Audrey Beckmann looked gravely at the two friends. 'You behaved recklessly and thoughtlessly,' she said seriously. She frowned at Josh. 'I know Olivia can't always help herself, but you're normally a little more sensible, Josh. And your brother expressly told you to stop interfering.'

Olly saw Josh squirm a little under her gran's keen gaze. 'We did get the stone back,' he said. 'You'd think people would be grateful,' he added sulkily, under his breath.

'You were lucky,' Olly's gran continued. 'You could have been hurt – or even killed. You are never to do anything so foolish again – do you understand me?'

'Yes, Gran,' Olly said quietly. Josh nodded.

The awkward interview was cut short by the sound of an approaching Land Rover.

'That's Dad!' Olly exclaimed.

They all came out of the trailer to meet the professor. His face was clouded as he climbed out of the Land Rover. He was clearly worried about Olly and Josh, but Olly quickly managed to convince him that they were both unhurt.

The recovery of the stone delighted the professor and he listened in amazement to Olly's description of the morning's events, and the chaos that had been caused by her activation of the tomb's booby-traps.

'The whole roof fell in!' Olly exclaimed, shaking her head. 'And just because I moved one little wedge. Those ancient Egyptians *really* didn't like burglars!'

'I hope there wasn't too much harm done,' her father said.

'The American and Habbib were a bit shaken up,' Olly replied. 'But the rest of us are fine.'

Her father blinked at her. 'I meant the tomb,' he said.

Olly grinned. Typical Dad!

Only a few minutes after Professor Christie's return, the police arrived to take Habbib and Benjamin Carter into custody.

'Let's hope this is an end to the matter,' Professor Christie said to the officers.

Olly noticed her dad staring at the American's wrist as he was put into the back of the police vehicle. And her father was silent and thoughtful as the police car drove away. 'What's wrong, Dad?' Olly asked.

He looked distractedly at her. 'That man had a tattoo on his wrist,' he said. 'It was the hieroglyphic symbol for Nuit.' He took out a small notepad and sketched a strange serpentine symbol.

Josh leant over Olly's shoulder to see. 'What's Nuit?' he asked.

'Nuit was the mother of Isis,' Olly said. 'I've read about her. She was the sky goddess who swallowed the stars every morning. She was also something to do with the whole resurrection business – they used to paint a picture of her inside the lid of a sarcophagus.'

'That's right,' said her father. 'She married the Earth god, Geb, son of Ra, and she gave birth to two sons, Set and Osiris, and two daughters, Nephthys and Isis.'

'Why would an American have a tattoo like that?' Josh asked.

'I have no idea,' replied the professor vaguely. He gazed towards Setiankhra's tomb. 'I must go and see what damage has been done,' he said. 'I hope all this trouble isn't going to slow down our work.' He slipped the note pad back into his pocket and headed for the tomb.

'I bet I can come up with plenty of explanations for that tattoo,' Olly said to Josh. 'For a start, that American might be a member of a secret cult, and—'

'I think we can leave the guessing games till later,' Olly's gran broke in, coming up suddenly behind the two friends. 'You're due some lessons about now.'

Olly stared at her. 'We found the Elephantine Stone, got two criminals locked up, and we *still* have to do lessons?' she said. 'Unbelievable!'

The friends spent much of the rest of the afternoon at their school work. They surfaced several hours later to find that, under Jonathan's supervision, a team of diggers had already constructed a temporary plank-built bridge over the chasm in the tomb. More lights had also been installed – the corridors and the burial chamber were now fully illuminated.

Josh and Olly walked carefully over the wooden bridge, peering down into the shadowy depths below where the wicked stone spikes waited.

'We almost ended up down there,' Josh remarked. 'Ouch!'

Olly nodded but said nothing, preferring not to think about it. Instead, she focused on the remarkable tomb decorations that the extra lights now revealed.

Despite the damage caused by centuries of flooding, the tomb was full of marvellous paintings – their colours bursting into life under the electric lights. The old dyes had held their intensity to an extraordinary degree. There were rich reds, emerald greens, splashes of pure white and pools of deep black. Hieroglyphics covered the spaces between the pictures – as Professor Christie had said only a few days ago, the secrets of Setiankhra's tomb looked like taking months of dedicated work to unravel.

Josh seemed preoccupied as he and Olly wandered back out into the late-afternoon sunlight.

'Are you wondering about Carter's tattoo?' Olly asked him. 'I am. I'm sure I've seen it somewhere before – only I can't remember where.'

Josh shook his head. 'No, it's something else,' he said thoughtfully. 'I didn't like to mention it in front of everyone, but I don't think Habbib was the same person we heard talking to Benjamin Carter in that store-room in Luxor.'

Olly frowned and tried to think back to what she had heard from her hiding place in the carpet. 'Now you mention it, I think you might be right,' she said. 'The Arab in Luxor sounded like a much younger man, didn't he?'

Josh nodded. 'He said he would meet up with Carter at the dig to hand over the stone, but what if he decided it was too risky to do it himself? What if he sent Habbib along instead?'

Olly's eyes widened. 'If that's right, you know what it means, don't you?'

Josh looked grim. 'It means the original thief could still be here – waiting for another chance,' he said.

'We have to tell my dad about this,' Olly declared. 'Come on!'

Confronted by Olly and Josh in his trailer a few minutes later, Professor Christie listened in concerned silence. 'I don't like the sound of that,' he said at last. 'I'll call the police and see what they have to say about it. In the meantime, Josh, would you go and find Jonathan for me? I was planning on asking him to drive up to Cairo in the morning and put the stone in a safety deposit box at the museum – but in view of what you've just told me, I'm going to suggest he drives up there tonight.'

Josh discovered Jonathan in their trailer, poring over old documents with the Elephantine Stone safely at his elbow. He agreed with the professor that the safest course of action was to get the stone as far from the camp as possible, and within the hour, he was waving goodbye as he set off in the Land Rover.

By the evening, the adventures of the day were beginning to tell on Josh and Olly. Not long after dinner, they grew tired of watching DVDs and decided to head for bed.

'Sleep well,' Olly's gran said. 'And remember

what I told you – no more stupid risks. Do you hear me?'

'Yes, Gran,' Olly yawned. 'I mean, no, Gran. I mean . . . oh, whatever you say, Gran.'

Olly said goodnight to Josh – who shared the trailer next door with his brother. Then she quickly got ready for bed, switched the light off and settled down between the sheets. She expected to be asleep in seconds, but her brain wouldn't shut down. It was as if a bright light was shining inside her head, and she couldn't turn it off.

She groaned, tossing and turning uncomfortably. In her head she could see the symbol of Nuit, mother of Isis, which her father had drawn earlier that afternoon. She had seen a tattoo just like that before – but when, and where?

Olly closed her eyes and desperately tried to remember. She had an image in her mind – simple, but very precise. She could see the ground at eye-level and a pair of feet under a long galabia robe. But whose feet? And why was the ground at her eye-level? Because she was in a hole, she realised suddenly. And with that, the memory came into focus.

It had been days ago. She had been helping the

diggers. She had been in a pit, shovelling earth into a basket, when someone had walked close to the edge, accidentally kicking sand down over her. Olly remembered standing up, ready to give them a piece of her mind – and then she had seen that it was Mohammed, the foreman. He had looked down and apologised profusely before moving away. And it was at that moment that Olly had briefly glimpsed the dark tattoo on the young man's bare ankle.

It was the serpentine symbol of Nuit. The same symbol that her dad had sketched earlier.

And the very same tattoo that Benjamin Carter had on his wrist.

Chapter Seven

Secrets Concealed and Secrets Revealed

Josh lay in pitch darkness, listening to the deep silence of the valley. He was stretched on his back, hands behind his head, thinking over the day's extraordinary events. Jonathan's bed was empty. It was a six-hour drive to Cairo, so the plan was for Jonathan to spend the night in a hotel and hand the stone over to the museum authorities first thing in the morning. He was expected back on site some time in the afternoon.

Josh was glad that the Elephantine Stone was gone. Far better that it should be safe on the road to Cairo than locked up in the small security box that Jonathan kept by his bed. Everyone on the site knew of the box – or could easily get to hear of it –

and Josh was certain that at least one thief was still at large.

He turned on to his side and began to drift off to sleep. But then he was shocked into wakefulness by a small, sharp sound. Josh opened his eyes in the darkness, his senses acutely alert. He was facing away from the door of the trailer, but he felt a breath of air on his cheek – as if the door was open.

Listening intently, his heart pounding, Josh heard the sound of stealthy footfalls moving slowly across the floor. Then he had the creepy sensation that someone was leaning over him. He thought it might be Jonathan, back early, but then dismissed that idea, realising it wasn't possible.

The next instant Josh guessed what was happening. The thief didn't know that the stone was gone – and he had come to Jonathan's trailer looking for it! Josh realised that this was his chance to discover the thief's identity. Summoning all his courage, he surged up from the bed, grasping the blanket and throwing it over the dark figure. There was a startled squawk as Josh's full weight came down on the intruder, bearing him to the ground. They tumbled together on to the floor, Josh on top, the thief enveloped in the folds of the blanket.

The thief struggled inside the blanket – and that was when Josh realised that something was wrong. The thief was too small!

Josh sat up, panting. He found the top of the blanket and pulled it off the face of his captive. 'Olly!' he exclaimed in surprise.

'You loon!' Olly gasped. 'What are you playing at?'

Josh rolled off her and switched on his bedside lamp. Olly stared up at him from the floor.

'I thought you were the thief,' Josh explained. He saw that she was fully clothed. 'What are you up to?' he asked.

Olly got up and sat on the bed. 'I've remembered where I've seen the Nuit tattoo before,' she told Josh. 'Mohammed has one exactly like it on his ankle.' And she explained how she had come to see it.

Josh looked thoughtfully at her. He shook his head. 'It's a coincidence,' he said. 'Mohammed's a really nice person – I can't see him stealing the stone. Besides, your dad trusts him completely, doesn't he?'

Olly nodded. 'He does,' she agreed. 'But right

now, that tattoo is the only lead we have. I think we should check it out.'

'We?' Josh asked dubiously, remembering Mrs Beckmann's stern words. 'Are you sure?'

'Dead sure!' Olly said. 'Come on, Josh, we're a great team. Look how well we did today. Are you with me or not?'

Josh nodded. 'Count me in,' he said, grinning. 'But what's our plan of action?'

'We need to find out whether Mohammed and Carter were working together, right?' Olly began. 'I thought we could wait till everyone's busy at the dig tomorrow, then take a look inside Mohammed's tent.'

'What do you think we'll find?'

'I'm not sure,' Olly replied. 'I doubt there'll be anything obvious – you know, like a diary with an incriminating entry: *Busy day today. Weather hot. Lots of digging. Stole Elephantine Stone*. Nothing like that. But I know Mohammed has a laptop computer and there might be something on that. He must have communicated with Benjamin Carter somehow – and e-mail would be the easiest way.'

'You're right,' Josh agreed, impressed. 'Good thinking!'

Olly grinned. 'OK, I'm off back to bed,' she said. 'See you in the morning.'

A few moments later, Josh watched from the window as Olly slipped back to her trailer through the quiet stillness of the desert night. It looked like tomorrow was going to be another eventful day, he thought – and if Olly's suspicions were correct, they might even find the evidence they needed to unmask the thief once and for all.

It was late the next morning when Olly and Josh sat down for breakfast with Olly's gran. They ate at a table set up by her trailer, shaded by a wide parasol. Mrs Beckmann was reading *The Times* – two days old – brought in from England.

Olly poured honey over the yoghurt and muesli mix in her bowl and stirred it thoughtfully with a spoon. Josh yawned a lot – still not fully recovered from the activity of the previous day.

Audrey Beckmann lowered her newspaper and peered at the two friends. 'So,' she said. 'Did you both sleep well?'

'Out like a light,' Olly said, not meeting her gaze. 'Straight to bed and straight to sleep, as per instructions.'

'Me, too,' Josh said. 'Has Jonathan phoned yet?'

'He spoke on the phone to Olly's father a couple of hours ago. He was about to take the stone into the museum. He said to expect him back some time mid-afternoon,' Olly's gran responded.

'Where's Dad?' Olly asked.

'Your father's been in Setiankhra's tomb for an hour or more already,' Mrs Beckmann said, nodding towards the distant entrance. 'And he was up studying old papers till the small hours last night.'

'Is Mohammed with him?' Olly asked innocently.

'I think so,' Mrs Beckmann replied. 'Your father took quite a big team over there.'

Olly looked significantly at Josh. The way was clear for them to put their plan into operation. She finished her breakfast and pushed the bowl away.

'I think I'll go for a stroll,' she said, stretching her arms above her head. 'Coming, Josh?'

'OK,' he said, bolting down the last of his breakfast. 'I'll be right with you.'

Mrs Beckmann looked at them. 'What are you two planning?' she asked.

'Nothing,' Olly said. 'You've got such a suspicious mind, Gran. Why should we be planning anything?'

Mrs Beckmann's eyebrows lifted. 'I meant, what do you intend to do with yourselves this morning?' she said.

'Oh.' Olly blinked at her. 'Nothing special. This and that.'

'Just remember what I told you,' her gran warned.

Olly and Josh looked at one another, and Josh tipped his head to indicate they should make their escape before Mrs Beckmann started asking more questions.

They had just left the table when one of the diggers, a cheerful young man called Fasal, came running from the tomb entrance. The professor wanted them. 'The professor – very excited,' Fasal explained, as the three of them followed him back to the tomb. 'He find writings – on wall. Very good writings – very important, he says.'

'It must be something to do with the Tears of Isis,' Olly murmured.

Professor Christie and Mohammed were in the burial chamber. The professor was crouched on the floor with a note pad on his knee, copying hieroglyphics from the wall, lit by a torch which Mohammed was holding.

Olly looked at the handsome young Egyptian. He met her eyes and smiled – and Olly felt slightly ashamed for suspecting him of stealing. Maybe her theory was a bit far-fetched.

Professor Christie stood up, his face eager and flushed. 'It was sheer luck,' he told them excitedly. 'I had only been working for a short time when I discovered this.' He pointed to the hieroglyphics.

Olly and Josh peered at them. So far as they could tell, the glyphs were no different to all the other enclosed writings that covered the walls of the chamber.

The professor pointed to part of the writing. 'This is the name of Nuit – not the single symbol we were talking about yesterday, that's just a kind of shorthand – this is the full name. It reads; "Nuit, mother of Isis, lays her blessings upon you, wise wanderer in the winding pathways of the world." ' His voice trembled with excitement. ' "I open the chambers of my heart to you." ' He turned to the three, his eyes shining. 'And then it says; "You who would gather the tears of my daughter, must first unlock the many doors of my house." Do you see? It must refer to the Tears of Isis – there's no other interpretation. The words in these hieroglyphs are intended to lead straight to that particular Talisman of the Moon!'

'Have you translated the rest?' Olly's gran asked.

'I have,' said the professor. He glanced down at his note pad. 'It seems to be in the form of a riddle.'

Mohammed spoke. 'My ancestors often hid their great secrets in riddles and puzzles,' he said. 'That way, only the wise and the worthy could understand them.'

'I'm good at riddles,' Josh said. 'What does it say?'

The professor read aloud from his notes. As he spoke, his voice seemed to grow stronger and deeper, booming through the empty chambers and echoing in the long corridors of stone.

' "In the Chamber of Light, the room that devours itself, the sacred two of the air, and the sacred four of the almond eyes, and the sacred six in the black armour shall unite beneath the sacred seven. And the light of the sacred seven will shine upon the head that is whole and the heart that is awake and the eyes that weep." '

A strange, breathless silence followed.

'Wow!' Olly said softly. 'That's amazing.'

'Could I have a copy of that?' Josh asked. 'I'd like to try and work it out, if I can.'

'Certainly,' the professor said. 'But even if you can solve the riddle, we're still left with another puzzle.'

'Let me guess,' Olly said. 'How do we find "the room that devours itself"?'

Her father nodded. 'Exactly.' He turned to Mohammed. 'We have more work to do,' he said. 'Let's hope our luck holds. At least we know one thing for certain: the clues on the Elephantine Stone were genuine – the Tears of Isis are apparently somewhere in this tomb!'

Olly and Josh walked towards the encampment where the tents belonging to Mohammed and several of the other diggers had been pitched. Those diggers who had been recruited locally – from Luxor, New Gurna and the nearby towns of Armant, Razagat and Qus – went home at nightfall. But at least a dozen diggers had come from as far away as Aswan or Cairo. They had formed a little camp near to the canteen run by Ahmed. It was hidden from the main excavation site by a thrusting shoulder of the hills.

'What do you think a room that devours itself can be?' Olly asked. 'It's just plain *weird*, if you ask me.'

'I don't know yet,' replied Josh. He frowned. 'But I've heard something like it before.'

'I've been thinking,' Olly said. 'What if the tattoos are a complete coincidence?'

'Then we won't find anything,' Josh said simply. He looked at Olly curiously. 'Have you changed your mind about searching Mohammed's tent?'

'Well, no,' Olly said, wavering. 'I suppose not. I just feel a bit awkward about it, that's all.' She chewed her lip thoughtfully. 'The tattoo *is* suspicious, though,' she said firmly. 'We ought to check it out. Let's get it over with.' She looked round – they were on the outskirts of the small camp. 'Which tent belongs to Mohammed?'

Josh pointed at the largest. 'That one,' he said.

'One of us should keep watch,' Olly suggested, looking back the way they had come. 'Are you OK with that, while I go and investigate?'

Josh nodded. 'I'll give you a call if I see anyone heading this way,' he said. He clambered up the hump of rock and peered over the top. From this vantage point he could see anyone coming in plenty of time. He turned and gave Olly the thumbs up.

Olly unzipped the flap of Mohammed's tent and crawled inside, pulling the zip down again behind her. The air was stuffy under the sloping canvas. A simple bed took up one side, and a few personal items sat on a small folding table: one or two books, shaving gear, an oil lamp. On the groundsheet, clothes and other basic items were laid out in neat piles.

Olly looked around quickly for the laptop. She found it on the bed, half-covered by a fold of the blanket. She drew it out and knelt on the floor to open it and switch it on. The screen lit up.

Olly felt uncomfortable – her conscience was still pricking her. What if Mohammed was totally innocent? What if she'd got it all wrong? 'He'll never know,' she whispered to herself firmly. 'Now I'm here, I might just as well get on with it.'

There were several folders and icons on the computer screen, most of which seemed to concern Mohammed's university studies, and similar archaeological and historical subjects. Olly rolled the mouse-ball and clicked on the envelope icon to run the e-mail program.

There were lots of e-mails in the inbox and they

had all been read. They came from various places – from individuals, from Cairo University and from several international museums as well. Olly was about to start reading them when a new e-mail arrived.

The sender was <u>ec@moon-phase.net</u>. She opened the mail. It was brief, with no greeting and no sign-off at the end.

How does your enterprise fare? Your ten per cent share in the venture is in jeopardy unless things are resolved quickly. I have other contacts willing to take over if you cannot fulfil your part of the deal. Respond immediately.

Olly raised an eyebrow. Someone out there wasn't very happy with Mohammed right now. He was obviously involved in a business deal that wasn't going smoothly. But was it anything to do with the Elephantine Stone? The e-mail was too vague for Olly to tell one way or the other.

Olly decided to read a few more mails. Now that she looked, there were several from the same address – <u>ec@moon-phase.net</u>. They might shed some light on the mystery.

But she didn't get a chance to read any other

e-mails because she was interrupted by a frantic voice from outside the tent. It was Josh. 'It's Mohammed!' she heard him call. 'He's coming! Olly, get out of there, now!'

Chapter Eight

The Riddle of Nuit

Josh had been daydreaming – gazing up at the cliffs and imagining what the Valley of the Kings must have been like at the time of the pharaohs. He hadn't thought for one moment that anyone would actually come over to the camp at this time of day. He had expected them all to be busy in the tomb. It was lucky that he happened to peer over the hump of rock and see Mohammed walking in his direction. The young Egyptian was already alarmingly close.

Panicking, Josh slid down the bulge of rock and raced for Mohammed's tent. He called a warning to Olly, then turned and sprinted back the way he had come. If he was quick, he would be able to head Mohammed off before he rounded the shoulder of rock. That would give Olly more time to make her getaway – and make up for not keeping a more careful watch.

In fact, Josh almost crashed into Mohammed and made him jump.

'Hello, there,' Josh said breathlessly.

'Hello, Josh,' Mohammed replied with a smile. 'You are in a hurry, I see.'

'Not really,' Josh began, thinking fast. 'Actually, I'm glad I bumped into you. I've been thinking about that riddle in the tomb. Do you have any idea what it might mean?'

'I've not had time to think about it,' Mohammed responded. 'But such things were the delight of my ancient ancestors. Far wiser men than I have spent entire lifetimes trying to solve the old riddles.' He smiled. 'This is an ancient country, Josh – its sands hide many secrets. Some may never be solved.' He nodded politely. 'Forgive me, I have to get something from my tent.' He sidestepped Josh and carried on.

Josh turned to walk alongside him. 'I could get it for you,' he offered.

'That's kind of you, but unnecessary,'

Mohammed said. 'It will only take me a moment.'

They were just outside the tent now. Mohammed stooped, drew up the zip and slipped inside. Josh closed his eyes, fearing disaster. But nothing happened. He opened his eyes again and saw something at the edge of his vision – a small, rapidly-moving shape. It was Olly, running at full pelt for the cover of the rocks. She had got out in time.

'Phew!' Olly gasped. 'That was close.' She looked at Josh, her eyes narrowing. 'How did that happen?' she demanded. 'You should have been able to see him from way off. I bet you weren't keeping proper watch!'

'Of course I was,' Josh answered defensively. 'Anyway, did you find the laptop?'

'I did,' Olly said. 'Although I only had time for a quick look.'

'Was there anything useful?' Josh asked.

Olly frowned. 'Not really. There was one e-mail that seemed a bit odd.' She explained about the mail from moon-phase.net. 'And there were others from the same person, but I didn't get a chance to look at them. When you yelled, I just had time to mark the mail as unread and put the laptop back where I found it.'

'So, we're no closer to finding out whether Mohammed and Carter were working together,' Josh mused. 'Maybe we should take another look in Mohammed's tent?'

Olly shook her head. 'I don't think that's such a great idea,' she said. 'We only just got away with it the first time. I'm still shaking!'

'So, what do we do now?' Josh asked.

'Let's get a copy of that riddle,' Olly suggested. 'If we put our heads together, we might be able to crack it.' She grinned at Josh. 'Wouldn't it be something if we worked out how to find the Tears of Isis before Dad and Jonathan?'

Olly and Josh sat at the table by the trailer, eating lunch. Each had a note pad and a pen. The translation of the riddle lay in the middle of the table.

> In the Chamber of Light, the room that
> devours itself, the sacred two of the air,
> and the sacred four of the almond eyes,
> and the sacred six in black armour shall
> unite beneath the sacred seven. And the

light of the sacred seven will shine upon
the head that is whole and the heart that
is awake and the eyes that weep.

Olly had been staring at the riddle for over half an hour, but no matter how hard she concentrated, the words refused to mean anything to her. She pushed her note pad away and sighed as she munched on an apple. 'This is giving me a headache,' she said. 'Face it – we're never going to work this out, even if we sit here for a million years!'

Josh looked up at her. He was smiling.

'What's funny?' she asked.

'You are,' he said. He tapped his pen on his pad. 'Look.'

Olly looked. Josh had drawn the rough shape of a snake, curled around into a ring with its tail in its mouth.

'Recognise that?' Josh asked.

'Yes,' Olly replied. 'It's like that symbol Dad showed us in the tomb.'

'And do you remember what he called it?' Josh continued, grinning. 'He said it was a picture of the snake that *devours* itself – an ancient symbol of eternity.'

Olly leant forward, interested now. 'So, a snake that devours itself is a snake eating its own tail,' she said. 'But how does a room eat its own tail? It doesn't make sense.'

Josh traced his pen around the snake-shape. 'See? It's a circle,' he said. 'Bet anything you like that "the room that devours itself" is a circular room.'

'Josh – sometimes you're almost brilliant!' Olly declared. 'That's got to be it. You've solved the first part of the riddle. At this rate, we'll have the whole thing worked out by dinner-time! I can't wait to tell Dad.'

'You can't wait to tell your dad what?' Mrs Beckmann asked as she came to join them.

Excitedly, Olly and Josh explained their theory about the circular room. She was obviously impressed. 'You're using your brains – I always approve of that – but I'm afraid you'll have to leave the rest for later,' she said. 'It's time for your lessons now.'

Olly frowned. 'But listen, Gran,' she said firmly. 'Seriously now, don't you think that solving this riddle is far more important than dull old lessons?'

'No,' her gran replied. 'I'll wait for you both in the trailer. Be there in five minutes.'

And that was the end of the conversation.

Jonathan had arrived back from Cairo by the time Olly and Josh emerged from their lessons. The Elephantine Stone had been successfully deposited in the museum – well out of reach of any other would-be thieves. And Jonathan had some additional news.

'We're to expect a special guest,' he said. 'She's in Italy at the moment, attending some film festival or other, but she'll be flying in to see us some time tomorrow.'

'Mum!' Josh shouted in delight.

Jonathan nodded, smiling. 'She called me on my mobile while I was driving back.' He winked at Olly. 'Things are going to be pretty lively around here for a while,' he said. 'You know what these Hollywood stars are like!'

A huge grin spread over Olly's face. If there was one thing that would make this Egyptian adventure perfect, it was a visit from Josh and Jonathan's glamorous movie-star mother, Natasha. She couldn't wait.

Josh and Olly were up early the next morning. At breakfast, Olly bombarded Jonathan with questions about Natasha Welles' visit, but he wasn't able to tell her very much more. She would be arriving some time that day, but she could only stay for a few hours, because she was needed back in Rome to start shooting her new movie – a thriller called *Cat's Cradle*.

'I expect she'll want a guided tour of the tomb,' Josh said. He looked at Professor Christie. 'Would that be OK?'

'It would be my pleasure,' replied the professor.

'I've got an idea for her next movie,' Olly said. 'It could be set in ancient Egypt, and she could play the female pharaoh, Nefertiti. She was supposed to be the most beautiful woman in the whole world at the time.'

Mohammed arrived and made a low bow. 'Excuse me, Professor, but I need your guidance over the clearing of the next chamber.'

'Of course, I'll be right along.' The professor drained his coffee cup and stood up. 'Come along, Jonathan. We've a busy day ahead of us.'

They hurried off with Mohammed, and Mrs

Beckmann started to clear the breakfast things. 'You and Josh can help me with this,' she said to Olly. 'And it's Saturday today – wash day – so I want all your laundry gathered together in the basket.'

Once their chores had been completed, Olly and Josh found themselves a good vantage point from which to watch the road. They were both impatient for the arrival of Josh's glamorous mother.

'What's that noise?' Olly asked, after half an hour without sighting a single car on the road.

Josh listened. It was an odd sound – a kind of distant throbbing. He stood up, shading his eyes to peer into the distance. He saw a dark pin-point in the sky and grinned. 'It's a helicopter,' he announced, with a laugh. 'Mum's arriving in a helicopter!'

The arrival of the helicopter at the archaeological dig caused a major stir. Word had already got around the camp that a Hollywood movie star was coming, and the diggers threw down their tools and crowded around as soon as the rotors stopped spinning, all of them eager to catch a glimpse of the celebrity.

Natasha Welles stepped down from the

helicopter, smiling and waving – every inch the movie star. Olly gazed at her in awe. Somehow Josh's mother always managed to look as if she was on a movie set – even now, when she was dressed only in jeans and a simple white blouse, with her long auburn hair tumbling loose down her back.

Josh and Olly pushed forwards through the crowds as a second figure appeared at the door of the helicopter. 'She's brought Ethan with her,' Josh remarked.

'Do you mind your mum bringing her latest boyfriend along?' Olly asked.

'No, Ethan's great,' Josh replied happily. He reached the front of the crowd and his mother opened her arms to greet him.

Olly knew about Ethan – anyone who read magazines, or watched TV, couldn't fail to know of Ethan Cain. He was a handsome, self-made millionaire, who had made his fortune from his computer company, and who now travelled the world as a modern-day adventurer. His name had been linked with Natasha Welles for several months now. There was even talk of a wedding, although both celebrities denied making long-term plans.

Ethan was also dressed casually in a shirt and jeans. He had piloted the helicopter.

Natasha shook hands and gave autographs and made her way gradually through the crowd, her arm around Josh's shoulders. Jonathan was waiting for her by the trailers. They hugged and Jonathan shook Ethan's hand.

'Trust you to make a spectacular entrance,' Jonathan said to his mother.

'You know me,' Natasha replied with a laugh. She hugged Olly and Mrs Beckmann. 'It's lovely to see you all again,' she said. She looked around. 'And what an amazing place this is. I'm so glad Ethan persuaded me to take time out and come down here.'

'There's lots to see,' Olly said. 'Do you want to visit the tomb? You'll never believe what's been going on – you see my dad found this old stone with—'

'For heaven's sake, let Natasha catch her breath,' said Mrs Beckmann. 'Come on into the trailer, I expect you could do with a rest and some lunch after your flight.'

Natasha put an arm around Olly's shoulders. 'Just let me get settled in, Olly,' she said. 'Then I want you to tell me everything that's happened.' She gave Josh and Jonathan a knowing look. 'My own children never tell me anything, so I'm relying on you to give me the full story.'

Olly and Josh had a great time over lunch. Ethan was friendly and funny, talking of white-water rafting in India and bungee jumping in New Zealand and scuba diving in Malaysia; his life seemed to be an endless series of exciting escapades. And Natasha clearly enjoyed being away from the pressures and expectations of her working life. She seemed happy and relaxed, and delighted Olly especially, by showing an interest in her adventures with Josh and chatting away like an old friend. The professor missed it altogether, he was so wrapped up in his work.

Both Natasha and Ethan were particularly fascinated by Josh and Olly's tale of the Elephantine Stone – its theft and spectacular recovery. Natasha laughed uproariously at Olly's description of her time inside the rolled-up carpet, and Ethan was riveted by the tale of the chaos caused when the ancient booby-traps were triggered.

'And right now,' Olly told them, 'we're working on a riddle that my dad found in the tomb.' She showed Ethan and Natasha the translation of the riddle. Ethan seemed particularly intrigued by it.

'I think the first part means a circular room,' Josh said, and explained his reasoning.

'Yes, I can follow that,' Ethan agreed. 'But what are the sacred, two, four and six?'

'We're still working on that,' Olly told him.

'It reminds me of the riddle of the Sphinx,' Ethan said thoughtfully.

'I know that one,' Josh put in. 'Initiates into the priesthood had to answer a riddle – what animal goes on four legs in the morning, two legs during the day and three legs in the evening? The answer is human beings. They crawl when they're babies – that's the morning of life. They walk upright as they grow up – that's the daytime of life. And they use a stick, like a third leg, when they're old – in the evening of life.' He looked at the riddle. 'So, do you think this could be similar?' he asked Ethan. 'Two – four – six. Do you think they're supposed to be legs?'

'Yes, that's it!' Olly said. 'A bird has two legs. Four legs would belong to some kind of land animal.' She frowned in concentration. 'And six legs has to mean an insect.'

'The Egyptians held the scarab beetle sacred,' Jonathan pointed out. 'That could be the answer. Two – four – six. Bird – animal – beetle.'

'And seven?' Natasha asked.

Olly grinned. 'An old beetle,' she joked. 'With a walking stick!'

Ethan laughed. 'I don't think so.'

Olly jumped up. 'Me, neither. But we've got most of it,' she said to Josh. 'We should go and tell Dad. He's going to be amazed!'

'And he might be able to help us make sense of the part about the sacred seven,' Josh added. 'We should ask him to take another look at the riddle on the wall of the burial chamber – I've got a feeling it might hold some more clues.'

Chapter Nine

Moon-phase

Ethan Cain and Natasha Welles gazed up in awe at the beautiful paintings that covered the walls of Setiankhra's tomb.

'They're breathtaking,' Natasha said, her voice hushed, her eyes wide. 'I never realised they would be so colourful – or so detailed.'

Olly smiled. 'They *are* pretty impressive,' she agreed. Then she turned back to Jonathan and her father, who were examining the hieroglyphs of the riddle. 'Have you found anything?' she asked. They seemed to have been scrutinising the glyphs and muttering quietly to each other for ages.

The professor stood up. 'I can't see anything to suggest what the sacred seven might be,' he said.

'There may be clues elsewhere, but it would take weeks to find them.'

'That's a pity,' Josh said. 'I suppose we'll just have to keep working on it.'

'But do you think we've got the rest right?' Olly asked her father. 'Is "the room that devours itself" a *circular* room?'

'It's a good theory,' Professor Christie agreed. 'Except for the fact that a circular room would be very unusual. The Egyptians seldom used curves in their architecture.'

Ethan stepped closer to the wall and looked at a hieroglyph to the left of the riddle.

'This bird image,' he said, 'it's a *benu*, isn't it?'

'Yes, a phoenix on a solar disc,' Jonathan replied, coming up alongside him. 'It's a frequent New Kingdom image.'

'There are similar images on the tomb of Ramses IV,' Ethan murmured. 'Have you worked out what it means in this context? Isn't that obelisk icon alongside it thought to be an embodiment of Osiris?'

'Yes, it is,' the professor confirmed. 'I had no idea you were interested in Egyptology, Mr Cain.'

'Please, call me Ethan,' he said. 'I'm no expert,

Professor; I'm just an enthusiastic amateur. But I have a few interesting items that I've collected over the years, and I enjoy the research.' He looked more closely. 'Have the writings in this cartouche been translated yet?' He examined the ancient brushstrokes. 'These symbols – they indicate "road", don't they?'

Jonathan nodded. 'Yes, the literal translation of this seems to be: "under me the backwards road" – but we have no idea what it means.'

'No.' Ethan's voice was soft. 'They certainly were a cryptic people.'

Natasha laughed. 'I know that tone, Ethan,' she said. She looked at Olly, standing at her side. 'It's the tone that gets into his voice just before he vanishes into one of his projects. It's a waste of time talking to him then – he's off in a world of his own.'

Olly nodded. 'Tell me about it,' she sympathised. 'Dad's just the same.'

Natasha put an arm around Olly's shoulders. 'Ethan, I'm going up top now,' she said. 'This place is incredible, but it's a little claustrophobic for my liking.'

Ethan, Jonathan and the professor were over at

the far wall, heads together, deep in conversation.

Natasha laughed. 'See what I mean?' she said to Olly. 'He's gone, already.' She smiled at Josh. 'Now then, do you two guys want to stay down here, or do you want to come with me and hear about my new movie?' For once, it was no contest. The three of them headed up the corridor to the surface.

'I want to hear all the latest Hollywood gossip,' Olly said to Natasha.

'I don't think there'll be time for *all* of it,' she replied, laughing. 'But I'll fill you in on all the best bits.' She looked over her shoulder. 'Josh, are you coming?'

The three of them had been walking along together, but Josh had suddenly stopped to stare at the wall.

'What is it?' Olly asked, walking back.

Josh was gazing at the depiction of the snake eating its own tail – the painting that had given him the idea of the circular room. He pointed to the stars that surrounded the snake. 'Remember the professor mentioning these?' Josh asked.

'Yes,' Olly replied. 'They're the Pleiades. Except that the ancient Egyptians called them something else.'

'The Krittikas,' Josh told her. 'Count them.'

'One, two, three, four, five, six – Oh!' Olly gasped. '*Seven!*'

'Seven sacred stars,' Josh agreed. '*Seven* – just like the riddle says.'

'We have to tell Dad,' Olly said excitedly.

'We can tell him when he comes up,' Josh said. 'After all, the riddle only tells us what to look for once we're in the room that devours itself. Jonathan and your dad still have to figure out how to find that room.'

Natasha was looking over their shoulders. 'I'm sure they'll work it out,' she said. 'And Ethan might even be able to help. He was being rather modest down there – he's really quite an expert on this stuff. He has several hundred items on display back home and a whole library full of reference books.'

Time flew for Olly and Josh as they sat with Olly's gran, drinking iced lemonade and listening to Natasha talk about her upcoming movie. It was mid-afternoon before Jonathan and Ethan emerged from the tomb and joined them under the parasol.

'Professor Christie is still down there,' Ethan said. 'He's busy translating more of the writing.'

'What have you people been doing?' Jonathan asked, pouring himself a glass of lemonade.

'Just chatting,' Olly said casually. 'Oh – and solving the last part of the riddle, as well.'

Jonathan stared at her. 'Excuse me?'

'We've figured out what the sacred seven are,' Josh told him gleefully. 'They're stars.'

'The Krittikas!' Ethan said, leaning forwards eagerly. 'Of course! A sacred bird, a sacred animal, a sacred scarab and seven sacred stars.' He laughed. 'You two are amazing!'

'Aren't we, though?' Olly said with a grin. She looked at Jonathan. 'Now all you and Dad have to do is find that room.'

'Easier said than done,' Jonathan replied. 'It could take six months to translate all the writings.'

'But the clues must be there,' Ethan said.

'I'm sure they are,' Jonathan agreed. 'Every aspect of the interment of a pharaoh had to be covered by protective spells – and every spell had to be written out in full. If the Tears of Isis were put in the tomb for safe-keeping, then spells will have been placed around them to protect them from desecration.'

'You mean by tomb-robbers?' Josh asked.

Jonathan nodded. 'But the spells weren't simply there to keep unwanted human marauders out,' he said. 'They were also there to stave off supernatural danger. The mythical world of the Egyptians was a dodgy place – if you didn't protect everything with very carefully-worded and detailed spells, all kinds of bad things could happen. The pharaoh could lose his way on his journey to the next world, or his food could be poisoned by demons, or his heart could literally be stolen from him! Getting from this world to the next wasn't easy.'

'I know you and Dad will find the Tears, eventually,' Olly said. 'And then they'll be put safely in a museum.' She noticed a frown cross Ethan's face as she spoke, but it soon cleared.

'Which museum will you donate the Tears to, if they're found?' he asked Jonathan.

'The Egyptian Museum in Cairo,' Jonathan replied. 'Professor Bey, the Museum Director, has been kind enough to give us full access for research purposes.'

'Natasha told me that you were on your way back from the museum when she called you,' Ethan went on. 'She said you put the Elephantine Stone there for safe-keeping. I wish I could have seen it before it was locked away – it sounds fascinating.'

'It's a shame I didn't call Jonathan before he handed it over,' Natasha remarked. 'I'm sure he'd have been happy to let you look at it.' She turned to Jonathan. 'Ethan was in Cairo, you know. That's where I met up with him to come down here. He's been there for several weeks.'

'I've been looking into a real estate deal,' Ethan said. 'I'm thinking of opening a branch of my company there.' He smiled. 'But that's boring stuff. Has Natasha told you about some of the stunts she'll have to do in the new movie? They're pretty wild.'

Josh looked impressed. 'You didn't say you were going to do your own stunts, Mum! What will they involve?'

Natasha laughed. 'Lots of hard work, I expect,' she said. And soon they were all enthralled by more tales of movie-making.

The afternoon sped away, and, all too soon for Josh and Olly, Natasha began to talk about the journey back to Rome.

'Can't you stop over just for one night?' Josh asked. 'It feels like you've only been here five minutes.'

'I know,' Natasha sighed. 'But I really can't. I have to catch a flight from Cairo to Rome tonight so that I can be at a press conference for noon tomorrow. Then I have a meeting with the producers, followed by a party at the Dei Borgognoni. I had to cancel several things to get away at all.'

'We still have another hour or so,' Ethan said. He looked at Olly and Josh. 'I've brought my camcorder with me, and I'd love to take some footage of the valley from the helicopter. I can't pilot the chopper and make a movie at the same time – would you two be interested in coming up with me to shoot some film?'

'You bet!' Josh said. 'I'll shoot the pictures.'

'And I could do a commentary,' Olly put in quickly.

Ethan smiled. 'That's fine with me,' he said.

Jonathan stayed with Natasha and Olly's gran, while Ethan led the two friends to the helicopter.

Once Josh and Olly were safely strapped in the back, Ethan climbed into the pilot's seat up front. Josh took command of the camcorder as Ethan gunned the engine. The noise rose to a steady, throbbing roar as the rotors began to turn – slowly and heavily at first, then faster and faster until they were just a dark blur.

Josh lifted the camera to his eye and pointed it out of the window to take some footage as the helicopter rose into the air.

'Whee-oo!' Josh whistled, as the land dropped quickly away below them. 'This is great – I'm going to have to ask Mum to buy me one of these for my birthday.'

'Which?' Olly asked. 'The camcorder or the helicopter?'

'Both!' Josh replied, laughing.

'Are you guys OK back there?' Ethan called.

'We're fine,' Olly shouted.

The helicopter circled and the landscape stretched out beneath them like a 3D map. The mountains flung long shadows across the rugged terrain in the early evening sunshine and the Nile sparkled like a thread of silver. The little river boats with their triangular lateen sails lay on the water like resting butterflies. Olly spied New Gurna, nestling among green fields, and across the river, small and remote, she made out the broken temples and narrow streets of Luxor.

Ethan banked the helicopter and turned to the

south, following the line of the valley. Olly leant close to Josh's shoulder to call out the names of the tombs as they flew over them.

'That one to the right – point the camera over there, Josh – that's Ramses the Fourth's tomb, and right ahead of us and to the left, is the tomb of the son of Ramses the Second. It's called KV5, and it's where Kent Weeks found a whole load of secret chambers,' Olly said.

'Just like we'll probably find in Setiankhra's tomb,' Josh added.

'Over to the left is the tomb of Ramses the Ninth,' Olly continued. 'And to the right is the tomb of Ramses the Second. And directly ahead of us is the tomb of Tutankhamen.'

The helicopter swept the length of the rugged valley, turning this way and that so that Josh could get clear shots of all the tomb entrances that pocked the craggy hills. The last tomb, deep in the shadow of overhanging cliffs, belongs to Tutmoses III.

Finally, Ethan swung the helicopter around and they headed north, back towards the excavation site.

'So, what turned you on to Egyptology, Ethan?' Josh asked.

'I suppose it was the remoteness and the grandeur of Egypt,' he replied. 'And the epic scale of it all – the complexity of the ancient civilisation.' A longing tone came into his voice. 'They were a great people. Imagine if you could go back there to watch the pyramids being built – to learn all those lost secrets first-hand.'

'Someone should invent a time-travel machine,' Josh said.

'Yes,' Ethan agreed. 'Someone should.'

The helicopter started flying in to land.

'And so,' Olly said, leaning over Josh's shoulder again, 'we return to the newly-discovered tomb of Setiankhra. Inside, even as I speak, the famous British archaeologist, Professor Kenneth Christie, and his assistant, Jonathan Welles, are working to decipher the cryptic clues left by the ancient people of this land, and find their way to the circular chamber that houses the Tears of Isis. Pictures supplied courtesy of Josh Welles. Your captain for this flight was Mr Ethan Cain. And this is Olivia Christie, signing off. Thank you for your attention.'

Josh lowered the camcorder as Ethan brought the helicopter down, amidst billowing clouds of dust.

'That was great,' Ethan declared. 'I loved the voice-over, Olly. Let's hope Josh got some good footage to complement it.'

'I'm sure I did,' said Josh.

They clambered out of the aircraft and began to make their way back towards the trailers, where Olly's gran, Jonathan and Natasha were still chatting.

'I just wanted to check that everything's OK for the flight back to Cairo,' Ethan called to the two friends. 'You go on ahead, I'll only be a few minutes.'

Olly turned and nodded, but as she looked back at the helicopter, something caught her eye. Behind the door to the fuselage, a logo was painted on the side of the aircraft. It was a silver oval, containing a silver crescent moon in one side and a silver full moon in the other. Beneath the logo, Olly read the word 'Moon-phase'.

'What's up?' Josh asked. He had stopped to wait for his friend.

Olly pointed at the logo. 'Moon-phase,' she said.

'That's right,' Josh agreed. 'I think it's a part of Ethan's computer firm. So what?' His eyes widened suddenly. 'Oh! I see the link – you're thinking of that e-mail on Mohammed's laptop, the one from moon-phase.net, aren't you?'

Olly nodded, momentarily speechless with surprise. The e-mail had come from <u>ec@moon-phase.net</u>. Could the 'ec' have stood for Ethan Cain? Olly wondered. Ethan Cain at Moon-phase?

Chapter Ten

The Hidden Door

Olly and Josh stared at each other. Olly felt as if the world had suddenly turned upside down and inside out. She couldn't be absolutely certain that the e-mails from moon-phase.net had been sent by Ethan – but if not, it was an extraordinary coincidence. But why would Ethan Cain be sending e-mails to Mohammed? Olly wondered. How could they even know each other? And, more to the point, exactly what kind of business venture would they be involved in together?

She looked again at the silver logo on the helicopter – and then back at Josh. 'We shouldn't say anything,' she murmured to him as they drew near the trailers. 'Not till we've had time to think about this.'

Josh nodded.

'I'll think of an excuse so we can get a few minutes on our own,' Olly whispered. Then she waved at Natasha, Jonathan and her gran. 'That was a great trip!' she called, as she and Josh walked over.

'Ethan's just checking the helicopter out,' Josh said.

Natasha sighed. 'Then we'll probably be on our way soon. What a pity. I'm having such a lovely time.'

'That voice-over was thirsty work,' Olly said. 'I'm going to get myself a drink. Would anyone else like one?'

'Just bring a jug of water out, please,' said Audrey Beckmann. 'And some fresh glasses.'

'I'll give you a hand,' Josh offered, and the two friends hurried inside together.

As soon as the door closed behind them, Olly turned to Josh. 'What on earth is going on around here?' she asked. 'Is everyone in the world trying to get their hands on the Elephantine Stone? Even Ethan?'

Josh opened the fridge and took out a large bottle of mineral water. 'It could all be perfectly innocent,' he said.

'Hmm,' Olly murmured dubiously. 'A coincidence that Mohammed and that American thug have the same tattoo? A coincidence that part of Ethan's company is called Moon-phase, and that Mohammed is getting e-mails from someone at moon-phase.net? A *coincidence* that all three of them happen to be in the same place at the same time?' She frowned. 'I don't think so!'

'But even if you're right about the e-mail, Ethan might be doing some perfectly ordinary business with Mohammed,' Josh suggested. 'After all, Mohammed's an archaeology student, and Ethan's interested in archaeology.'

Olly shook her head. 'In which case, why hasn't Ethan mentioned that he knows Mohammed?' she asked. 'Do you want to know what I think? I think Ethan's got something to do with the Elephantine Stone being stolen.'

Josh shook his head. 'He wouldn't do something like that,' he protested. 'He's a millionaire. If he wants something, he can just buy it – he doesn't have to steal stuff.'

'He can't buy stuff that isn't for sale,' Olly pointed out. 'And the Elephantine Stone *definitely* isn't for sale. And I've just remembered something

– Carter said he had a buyer lined up for the stone in Cairo. And Ethan has been in Cairo for the past few weeks, hasn't he?'

Josh stared at her. 'You think Ethan was the *buyer*?' he gasped.

Olly nodded as a pattern began to form in her mind. 'Maybe Mohammed and Carter were both working for Ethan,' she breathed. 'Mohammed's job was to steal the stone and hand it over to Carter. Then Carter was supposed to take it to Cairo and give it to Ethan. But it all went pear-shaped when *we* overheard Carter's plans and got the stone back!'

'That might have been why Ethan suggested to Mum that they come and visit us down here,' Josh added. 'Maybe he had an ulterior motive.' Then he shook his head. 'But Ethan seems like a really great person. There has to be another explanation.'

'Are you sure about that?' Olly asked grimly. 'Ethan's pretty charming on the outside – but what's he like deep down?'

Josh gazed at her, temporarily lost for words. 'Even if we're right,' he said at last, 'we can't just go and tell everyone. They'll think we're out of our minds. Mum really likes Ethan – she's never going to believe he's involved in stealing the stone.'

'True,' Olly agreed thoughtfully. 'And if we do say anything, Ethan and Mohammed will just deny it and we'll end up looking like idiots.' Her forehead creased in concentration. 'Maybe we're just jumping to conclusions,' she said. 'After all, Ethan knew the stone was safely locked away in Cairo before he came here. Your mum told him, remember? So, why fly down here when the stone has already gone?'

'Perhaps he wants something else,' Josh suggested slowly. 'After all, your father and Jonathan are using the stone to help them find a bigger treasure. Perhaps Ethan has the same thing in mind.'

Olly gaped at him. 'You think he wants the Tears of Isis?'

'Could be,' Josh replied. 'Mum said he has a big collection of artefacts – maybe he wants to add the Tears to it.'

That made sense to Olly – the Tears of Isis would be a major addition to any collection. 'But they're leaving soon,' she said. 'If he was hoping to find the Tears, he'd need to stay here longer than one single day.'

'Yes, but—' Whatever Josh had been intending to

say was interrupted by the sound of the trailer door being opened from the outside.

Ethan appeared in the doorway. 'I'll have some water, please, guys,' he said. 'Although I could use something a little stronger!'

Olly hastily poured the mineral water into a jug, while Josh got out the glasses. 'Is there a problem?' she asked.

Ethan nodded. 'There's a fault with the chopper's engine,' he said. 'We were lucky it didn't show till we were back on the ground. I'm going to have to send for a replacement part.' He smiled ruefully. 'It looks like we're going to be imposing on your hospitality a little longer than expected. Natasha is going to make some calls and reorganise her schedule. Jonathan will drive her back to Cairo in the morning, while I'll be staying here till the engine part arrives. But hey, every cloud has a silver lining – it'll give me more time to explore the tomb.' He gave them a friendly wink. 'You never know, I might even be able to help the professor find the room that devours itself.'

He took the bottle of water from Olly's hands and left the trailer.

Olly looked at Josh. 'I bet there's nothing wrong

with the helicopter,' she hissed. 'It's just an excuse for him to stay on.' Her eyes narrowed determinedly. 'We're going to have to watch him every minute, day and night.'

Josh nodded. 'You're right. Poor Mum,' he said. 'She really likes him.'

'Well, he's a rat,' Olly said firmly. 'And we're going to do everything we can to *prove* that he's a rat!'

It was early evening, and long shadows were reaching out across the valley. The sun had dipped behind the western cliffs, but the sky was still bright. There were another two hours till dusk.

Olly and Josh were sitting at the table with Olly's gran, Josh's mother and Ethan Cain. Natasha had just finished a call to her agent in Hollywood. She flipped her mobile shut. 'Judy is going to see that everything is reorganised for me,' she told them. 'If Jonathan and I head off early in the morning, I should still be able to catch the mid-afternoon plane from Cairo to Rome.' She smiled at Olly. 'Meanwhile, you can tell me more about that movie idea you have for me. Who would I be playing?'

'Nefertiti,' Olly told her. 'She was a really beautiful pharaoh.'

'If you're going to talk movies, I think I'll go and stretch my legs,' Ethan said. He got up. 'I'd like to see how Jonathan and the professor are getting on in the tomb.'

The diggers were only employed for a half-day on Saturday, but Olly's father and his assistant had decided to do some more exploring on their own. There was plenty of work to be done in Setiankhra's tomb that didn't require hired labourers.

Olly and Josh watched Ethan as he strolled past the trailers and turned out of sight at the end of the row.

'I think I'll go for a walk, too,' Josh said, standing up.

'And me,' Olly added.

Natasha gazed at them with a crooked smile. 'Everyone's abandoning me,' she wailed. 'Was it something I said?'

'Don't mind them,' Audrey Beckmann commented. 'They can't keep still for five minutes.' She looked at the two friends. 'Don't lose track of the time,' she said. 'I'll be starting dinner in an hour or so. I want you back here, washed and ready to eat by eight.'

'OK,' Olly agreed. She smiled at Natasha. 'We can talk about the movie over dinner. I've had some great ideas.'

'I'll look forward to that,' Natasha replied.

Josh and Olly wandered off after Ethan. 'We can't just follow him,' Josh whispered to Olly. 'He'll see us.'

'I know,' Olly whispered back. 'This way.' Josh followed, and within moments, they were peering out of the back of the trailers.

'There he is,' Olly whispered.

Ethan was heading towards the tomb entrance.

'Maybe he really *is* just going to see how Jonathan and your dad are getting on,' Josh suggested.

Olly wasn't so sure. 'Wait!' she hissed.

Her suspicions were proved correct. Halfway to the tomb, Ethan gave a quick glance over his shoulder and then turned and strode briskly in the opposite direction – away from the tomb and towards the campsite.

'Got him!' Olly whispered sharply. 'I bet he's off to talk to Mohammed.'

The friends followed Ethan carefully, keeping

low and sticking to the shadows as much as possible. It meant he got well ahead of them, but at least he didn't realise he was being tracked.

He rounded the shoulder of rock and disappeared from sight. Josh and Olly raced after him, scrambling up the side of the rocky outcrop.

'Keep your head down,' Josh warned as they neared the crest of the ridge. They both peered cautiously over the top and Olly let out a soft hiss of satisfaction.

Ethan Cain was only a few metres away from them – and Mohammed was with him. The two men were speaking together in low voices. The urgent murmurings drifted up to the friends, but neither of them could pick out any of the actual words. However, one thing was very clear from the tone of the men's voices and the way they were behaving – Ethan was angry and Mohammed was trying to soothe him.

Their conversation lasted only a minute or so. Mohammed gestured back the way Ethan had come. Ethan nodded sharply and the two men turned and headed back together.

Olly and Josh flattened themselves against the rocks. They were well above the men, and unless either of them happened to glance upwards, there was a good chance that the two friends wouldn't be spotted.

Olly watched as Ethan and Mohammed passed them and made their way towards the tomb. Mohammed was carrying a large torch.

'What do you think they're up to?' Josh whispered.

'No good, that's for sure,' Olly replied. 'Let's go.'

They kept their distance as they trailed their quarry. The men were walking quickly, both of them looking round every now and then, as if to check they weren't being observed. Olly and Josh's pursuit consisted of wild dashes from one piece of cover to the next. It wasn't long before the men were a good way ahead of them – but they daren't draw any closer for fear of being seen.

Olly watched from the shadows of a long, low rock as Mohammed and Ethan entered the tomb of Setiankhra. 'I wish we could have heard what they were talking about,' she said. 'What if they're just going down there to see how Dad and Jonathan are doing? That won't prove anything!'

'There's only one way to find out,' Josh said. 'Come on.'

He ran the last twenty metres to the tomb with Olly close behind. The entrance showed up clearly – a flare of electric light in the gathering dusk. 'Slowly now,' Josh murmured.

Olly nodded.

They stepped into the tomb, moving as quietly as possible, both of them listening intently for any tell-tale sounds of the two men. Silently, they crept across the wooden bridge and down the second corridor. As they neared the bottom, they heard voices.

Olly paused, her heart pounding.

Josh looked at her and put his finger to his lips. They pressed themselves against the wall and edged a little closer to the entrance of the burial chamber.

'They've found it!' It was Ethan's voice, quiet but excited.

'They must have gone through,' Mohammed said.

Olly came to the entrance and peeped round the corner. There was no sign of Jonathan, or her father, but she could plainly see Ethan and Mohammed. The two men were standing together at the far end of the chamber. But it was something else which completely took her breath away.

Where previously the wall of the chamber had been smooth and flat, there was now a rectangular opening, about a metre wide and slightly more than a metre high. It was just below the place where the professor had pointed out the hieroglyphics that mentioned Nuit.

Olly's heart pounded. Her father and Jonathan had somehow found the hidden doorway! As Mohammed had said, they must have gone through to explore because there was no sign of them on this side.

'I had no idea they were so close to finding the hidden entrance,' Ethan remarked. 'We must follow them.'

Mohammed gripped Ethan's arm as the computer genius moved to go through the door. His voice was suddenly low and urgent. 'Look!' he said, pointing to the writings over the door. 'Do you see the hieroglyphs?'

'I don't have time to translate,' Ethan snapped. 'What do they say?'

Mohammed moved closer to the wall. Something in his voice sent shivers up Olly's spine as he translated aloud. ' "This shall be the gift of Nuit to thee, traveller on the backwards road. Thou shalt not die. Thou shalt move through all the ages. Thou shalt have one foot in the future and one foot in the past. Deathless traveller, thou shalt live for a million million years." '

Ethan let out a slow, triumphant breath. 'Ahhhh!' He gripped Mohammed's shoulder. 'Just as I'd hoped!'

But Mohammed backed away from the wall, his eyes uneasy. 'I will not go through there,' he said. 'The danger is too great. Night is coming – and a powerful moon is rising. This is not the time to desecrate a tomb protected by Nuit.' He shivered, staring around warily. 'I feel her presence all around me in this place,' he muttered. Then he turned and looked intently at Ethan. 'There's still time to give this up – to go away from here and forget.'

Ethan moved purposefully towards him. 'Forget?' he murmured. 'Forget something I've been searching for all my life? I don't think so.'

'Then you must travel the road alone,' Mohammed told him. 'I will have nothing more to do with it.' He turned and headed back towards the corridor to the surface.

Olly flinched away, treading on Josh's feet as she

tried to keep out of Mohammed's sight. Josh caught her hand and drew her quickly into one of the side-chambers.

'I'm going through the doorway,' they heard Ethan snarl at Mohammed. 'And I need you to come with me.'

Mohammed walked past the entrance to the side-chamber and further on along the corridor. 'No, not tonight,' he said. 'It isn't safe.' The writings on the wall had clearly unnerved him.

Olly saw Ethan stride hurriedly after Mohammed. She sidled to the entrance of the chamber and peered out.

Ethan had caught up with Mohammed just a little further up the passage. 'Think about what we might find!' he said, his voice urgent and persuasive. 'Are you really prepared to miss out on the opportunity of finding the Tears of Isis?'

The Egyptian's footsteps faltered. Ethan's words had obviously had an effect on him. He turned back uncertainly. And then he caught sight of Olly!

Ethan must have seen the recognition in Mohammed's eyes, for he whirled round, then lunged at Olly.

'Josh! Time to get out of here!' Olly yelled,

running away from Ethan and down into the burial chamber. Josh raced after her, with both Ethan and Mohammed close on his tail.

The friends tumbled into the stone chamber as an angry shout from Ethan echoed off the walls behind them. They were trapped – there was only one way out!

Olly caught hold of Josh's sleeve and dragged him through the black doorway in the chamber's wall. 'Help me!' she gasped. And, together, she and Josh heaved the heavy stone doorway closed, just as Ethan hurled himself towards it.

In spite of Ethan's momentum, the door thudded shut, plunging Olly and Josh into deep, impenetrable darkness.

Chapter Eleven

Secrets of the Tomb

A thin beam of bright light cut suddenly through the darkness. Josh had pulled a small torch from his pocket. The light illuminated a grey stone wall and a floor strewn with rubble. They were in a narrow corridor which stretched away to the left and right, parallel to the burial chamber.

'We need to find Dad,' Olly said.

Josh raked the beam of light along the featureless corridor in both directions. 'Which way?' he asked.

They heard the grinding sound of stone grating on stone. Josh aimed the torch at the doorway. It was being pushed open from the outside.

Olly didn't wait to think. 'This way!' she said, running to the left.

Josh followed, taking a quick look over his shoulder as he ran. He saw a crack of light in the wall – Ethan and Mohammed would soon have the door open again.

Olly was in the lead. 'Give me the torch!' she gasped. Josh handed it over. Olly grazed one hand along the wall as the thin white beam stretched out ahead of them, lighting up the rough floor and the narrow grey walls.

A black slit appeared in the wall to their right. They ran past it. There was another, and another – dark passageways leading off at right angles to the main corridor.

A flare of light behind them threw their shadows forwards. They were caught in the bright beam of a powerful torch. Ethan and Mohammed were chasing them along the corridor.

Olly caught hold of Josh's arm and pulled him into one of the side-passages. This new corridor was exactly the same as the other – a straight, grey tunnel, little more than shoulder-width, and around two metres high.

But then they came to something different. A small chamber. Olly shone the torch around. The walls were covered with intricate paintings. Animal-headed figures sat in profile on chairs, watching as a jackal-headed figure – that Olly recognised as Anubis – weighed a human heart against a feather on a set of simple scales. The crocodile-headed god, Thoth, waited nearby. Olly knew his task – to gobble down any hearts that failed the test. Screeds of hieroglyphs filled the spaces between the paintings.

'Wow!' Olly breathed.

'No time for "wow",' Josh panted. 'Which way out?' Five identical tunnels led off in every direction, like spokes from the hub of a wheel.

'Beats me,' Olly gasped. She tried to go over their route in her head. Left from the doorway, then a right had brought them here. If they wanted to work their way back round to the doorway in the burial chamber, then she figured they should go right and right again. Hopefully, that would take them full circle.

Olly flashed the light into the tunnel that led off to the right. 'This one!' she said.

They ran along the stone passage, deeper and deeper into the heart of the mountains. Olly noticed that the walls here were inlaid with green jasper. And painted cobras, with gleaming jewelled eyes, reared up the corridor walls.

The friends came to a sharp bend. The wall ahead was covered in a huge painting of the god Osiris, holding a crook and flail. His wife, Isis, stood behind him, and ahead of them were the four sons of Horus.

In spite of the fear of pursuit, Olly had to be dragged away from the wall-painting. She had spent all her life learning about ancient Egypt from her father – and now she was seeing incredible masterpieces that had lain hidden and lost for thousands of years. It felt to Olly as if they were running through a kaleidoscope of Egyptian mythology – going ever deeper into a dead world that their presence was bringing back to life.

'We're going down,' Josh commented.

'I know,' Olly replied. The tunnel had been sloping for some way now. Olly didn't like to think of how far under the surface they must be. 'Not again!' she gasped.

They had come to another chamber with six exits leading out of it. Here, the paintings depicted green boats sailing across an azure sky. Seated in the largest boat was a man with a scarab for a head. A lion lay – sphinx-like – shaded by papyrus plants that were entwined with cobras. The eye of Horus stared down from above every entrance.

Again, Olly chose the tunnel to the right. If her mental picture of the place was accurate, she thought they should now be heading back to the main part of the tomb. There was only one problem – how deep under the ground were they now? The passage ran level for some time, but then it dipped alarmingly, shooting down like a ramp into a well of darkness.

Olly pointed the torch down, but the tunnel fell away beyond the beam. 'This can't be right,' she panted. 'We're too deep. We should go back and find a passageway that heads upwards.'

Josh stared back up the tunnel. 'Can I have the torch?' he asked.

Olly handed it to him. He sent the beam skidding back the way they had come. A thousand almond-shaped eyes glittered at them from the walls. 'Listen!' Josh said.

Olly held her breath and strained her ears.

'Hear it?' he asked.

She nodded. It was distant, but unmistakable – the sound of feet pounding on stone, echoing down through the corridors and chambers. Ethan and Mohammed were still in pursuit.

'We can't go back,' Josh said. 'We might run straight into them.'

'Were are Jonathan and Dad?' Olly wailed.

'They must have gone another way,' Josh said. 'There were lots of side-tunnels – they could be anywhere!'

'Great!' Olly took a deep breath. 'We'd better go on then,' she decided.

They hurried on, side by side, down the slope. The corridor tilted as steeply as a child's slide, making it difficult for Josh and Olly to keep on their feet. Then Olly brought her heel down on a piece of loose stone that skidded away beneath her. She slipped and fell against Josh, and soon they were both sliding down the shaft, the torch-light skimming the walls and ceiling as they plunged downwards.

Their fall was halted by a bank of loose, dry sand and rubble. They tumbled into it, breathless and bruised. It was a few moments before Olly could catch her breath enough to speak. 'Are you OK?' she asked.

'I think so.' Josh groaned, sitting up. Sand cascaded off his clothes. He shone the torch beam around them. 'Look at that.' He pointed the beam at the top of the bank of sand and stones where it reached the ceiling of the passage. The roof had fallen in and the heaped sand and rubble was the result of the collapse. 'It's completely blocked!' Josh said. 'We'll never get through. And listen . . .'

Again, they could hear the tell-tale sounds of pursuit. And now, mixed in with the echoing footfalls, they could also hear voices – weirdly distorted – drifting down the long slope towards them.

'Well, we can't go back,' Olly said. 'Shine the light here.' Josh turned the torch beam back on to the sand and rubble. Olly crawled up to where the debris met the roof and began to dig, scooping out the sand and throwing the lumps of stone down behind her.

'What are you doing?' Josh asked.

'What does it look like?'

'But the tunnel could be blocked for another twenty metres!' Josh pointed out.

Olly ignored him. She was working hard, shovelling the sand away with both hands.

Josh shook his head. 'This is crazy,' he sighed. But he scrambled up the slope and joined Olly, holding the torch between his teeth and using his hands to dig away the sand and rock.

The pair worked in dogged silence for some minutes. Sweat was pouring off them on to the sand and they were both gasping for breath. They had moved forwards about a metre, and then, quite suddenly, Olly wrenched a lump of stone away and found a hole. They had reached the place where the roof had caved in.

They renewed their efforts, revealing a broken-edged gap that expanded to the full width of the roof. Olly took the torch and squirmed up through the hole. 'It goes up about two metres,' she called down to Josh. 'I can see exits to either side – and a roof. I think it's another passage running right above this one!'

They cleared away more debris and soon stood side by side in the hole.

'Cup your hands,' Olly said. 'Help me climb up.'

Half a minute later, the two friends were standing in the higher tunnel. Josh had the torch now. He played the beam to the right. 'Uh-oh!' he said. This corridor ended in a flat stone wall, about twelve metres away. He turned the beam the other way and sighed with relief. The tunnel continued ahead for twenty metres or so, then there was a black square – an entrance or an exit.

The friends hurried on together, and stepped through the entrance. They found themselves standing on a platform of white stone slabs, flanked by life-sized shabti warriors made of shining quartz crystal. Josh moved the torch beam around the chamber they had entered. It was huge, the roof soaring up and away in a high arch of faintly glowing white rock. Olly saw that the walls were carved with bas-relief depictions of the soul's journey to the afterlife.

Two immense stone columns, decorated with carved palm-fronds, held the roof up. At the base of each pillar sat a huge black statue – at least three metres tall – of Osiris, the god who watched over the netherworld. Next to him sat a statue of his son, Horus, with a falcon's head and eyes of gold and silver – to represent the sun and the full moon.

Behind these two majestic gods, a vast chasm opened up, splitting the chamber in two.

'Can you believe this?' Olly murmured as she slowly crossed the chamber.

Josh didn't reply. He was gazing round in awe.

They walked together to the edge of the chasm. Josh pointed the torch at the far side – it was easily five metres away. The light also revealed a slender stone bridge, spanning the gulf, just wide enough for a person to cross. There was no hand-rail or support. Beyond the bridge was another platform of white stones, and a dark, square gateway in the far wall of the chamber, also guarded by shabti warriors. Their green, jewelled eyes glinted menacingly in the torchlight.

Josh stepped forwards and shone the torch down into the chasm. Many metres below, he saw a forest of sharpened stone spikes, and with a shudder, he noticed that human skeletons lay among them. He looked at Olly. 'That's not a comforting sight,' he said quietly.

Olly pursed her lips and stared at the thin stone bridge. 'We can do it,' she said. She glanced at Josh. 'Do heights bother you?'

'Do they bother *you*?' he returned.

Olly shook her head.

'That's good, then,' Josh said firmly. 'I'll go first.'

Olly nodded and Josh stepped carefully out on to the bridge. He shone the light down at his feet. Olly swallowed hard, trying not to think about the spikes and skeletons below as she edged on to the bridge behind him. The stonework was narrow and smooth, but it looked safe.

Slowly they approached the middle of the bridge. 'How are you doing?' Olly asked, surprised to find that her voice was shaking.

'It's easier than I expected,' Josh replied. 'And by the way – I *don't* like heights.'

Olly smiled. 'You're doing fine,' she told him.

'Thanks,' Josh said, glancing over his shoulder. But it was a bad move. Momentarily distracted, Josh stumbled. Olly reached forwards to catch him as he tripped, but she missed. He fell hard. His fingers managed to catch the bridge, but the torch fell from his hand.

Olly watched in horror as it plummeted into the chasm.

Chapter Twelve

The Golden Doors

Josh heard a crack as the torch hit stone somewhere far below, and then the chamber was lost in utter blackness. He lay, sprawled on the cold stone bridge, face down, his heart hammering. His fingers gripped the edges of the bridge while his mind whirled. He had dropped the torch! They were lost and blind and a single, ill-judged movement could send them plunging down to the deadly spikes below.

He felt Olly's hands on his legs and heard her voice. 'Josh – are you OK?' she asked.

'Yes. You?' he answered.

'I'm fine,' Olly replied. 'But we need to get off this bridge.' Josh knew she must be terrified, but her voice sounded calm. 'I'm going to back up. We'll just have to hope Ethan and Mohammed find us. At least they've got a torch. We'll never get out of here without a light.'

'No.' Josh felt himself grow calmer. His brain was beginning to work again. 'Stay where you are.' He rose cautiously to his hands and knees and then sat back on his heels. He fumbled in his pockets until his fingers found the piece of candle and box of matches he always carried with him.

His hands trembled as he opened the box and struck a match. The light flared and grew steady. Josh touched the match to the candlewick, which caught and burned brightly. He was pleased by how strong the flame was. Now he could see the ground at his feet – though the shadows hemmed him in on all sides.

He turned. Olly was staring at him, her eyes bright in the candlelight. 'You carry a candle?' she asked incredulously.

Josh nodded. 'Jonathan gave it to me. He always carries matches and a piece of candle in the tombs. Just in case.'

'Clever,' Olly said. 'Remind me to thank him. Shall we get across this bridge now?'

Very carefully, the pair made their way to the far side of the chasm. Josh felt an overwhelming sense of relief when he finally stepped off the narrow bridge. He lifted the candle to see the exit from the chamber and headed towards it. Olly followed, and the dark raced in behind her, as though it was giving chase.

Beyond the exit, the tunnel was no more than three metres long. It opened into another chamber so huge that Josh and Olly couldn't see the far walls or the roof. On either side of the entrance stood massive obsidian statues, each with the head of a hawk.

'That's Horus,' Olly remarked nervously as she gazed up into the god's fierce face. The statues' black eyes stared out over Olly's head, their haughty gaze fixed eternally on the engulfing darkness. She touched the cold, shining stone of one of the statues. 'When was the last time anyone saw this?' she murmured. 'It must have been thousands of years ago.'

Josh raised the candle. The walls that stretched away on either side of the entrance were covered with immense bas-relief sculptures, depicting mythical scenes of gods and men and animals.

Their colours shone in the flickering candlelight – red and gold and green, blue and yellow and white, eventually disappearing into the darkness.

Awed by the vastness of the place, Josh and Olly moved further into the room. And then they both gasped in wonder and disbelief, because piled around the towering pillars that supported the roof, lay golden treasures! Plates and jewelled goblets, statuettes and swords, shields and bowls, all glittered and gleamed and threw back the candlelight.

Josh's head spun with the wonder of it all. He felt small and insignificant among such wealth and beauty and grandeur. The light of the candle seemed a tiny flicker in that great lost hall of treasures.

'It's as if they're watching us,' Olly said, her voice low with awe.

Josh turned and saw that she was referring to two great statues of Isis that had emerged from the gloom ahead of them. They *did* seem almost alive, he thought. As if at any moment a head would turn and a hand lift, creaking with the weight of years. It was scary, but it was wonderful at the same time.

They walked between them and found

themselves in a colonnade of warrior statues, all facing inwards. A wall appeared at the end of the guarded aisle. It was covered in richly-coloured paintings. This time, all the people and animals were facing to the right.

'It's like a kind of procession,' Olly said, approaching the painting. 'I wonder where they're all going.'

The wall arced, and Olly followed the painted procession around the curve. 'Josh?' Olly's voice was breathless with excitement. 'This is a curved wall!'

'Yes, I noticed,' Josh replied. He knew what Olly was thinking – the same thought had occurred to him. Did the wall form a circle? And if so, what lay inside?

The procession ended. Two women in white robes knelt at the feet of a tall figure with the head of a jackal – the god Anubis. At his back was a mass of hieroglyphic writings. And beyond that was a pair of huge, closed doors, made of gleaming, beaten gold. Josh could see a rippled reflection of his own face in the shiny metal.

For some time, the friends simply stood, staring up at the golden doors, speechless with amazement

– all thought of their pursuers forgotten. Olly was the first to break the silence. 'I think this is it,' she whispered reverently. 'I think we've found the room that devours itself!'

Chapter Thirteen

The Chamber of Light

'How do we get in?' Olly breathed, staring up at the doors.

Josh held the candle closer, searching for a handle or a lever. There was nothing. The candle guttered and a rivulet of hot wax burned his fingers. He looked down anxiously. The candle was already half-eaten away by the flame. It wouldn't be much longer before it became too short to hold. And then what? He had matches, but they were only good for a few seconds each. And once the matches were gone, the darkness would swallow them whole, and that would probably be the end of them. He decided not to share his thoughts with Olly.

She was moving to and fro, running her hands over the doors, as if hoping to find something invisible to the eye. She pushed against them. They didn't move. 'There has to be a way of getting them open,' she said.

'Open sesame!' Josh intoned solemnly. Nothing happened.

'As if!' Olly said, dropping to her knees. 'Give me some light.'

Josh crouched beside her. She was at the join between the doors. Here, the stone floor had been hollowed out to make a small hole. Olly pushed her fingers in under the doors. 'I can feel something,' she said. 'It's hard and sharp and—' There was a loud metallic click and Olly saw the doors shiver slightly. She stood up and pressed her hand against them. They creaked open slowly.

Together, the two friends moved forwards into the room, all thought of danger temporarily forgotten in astonishment and delight. The room was like the inside of a huge golden bell. The enclosing walls and the vaulting ceiling were made of panels of highly-polished gold, which glowed dark yellow in the candle flame. The panels were etched all over with fine drawings and writings.

Even the floor was gold. Josh could see his topsy-turvy reflection when he looked down. 'Wow!' he breathed.

Olly looked at him, her eyes shining. 'How did the riddle go?'

'In the Chamber of Light, the room that devours itself, the sacred two of the air, the sacred four of the almond eyes, and the sacred six in black armour shall unite beneath the sacred seven,' Josh recited. 'And the light of the sacred seven will shine upon the head that is whole and the heart that is awake and the eyes that weep.'

'OK, we think the two and the four and the six represent legs, and the seven are the Pleiades,' Olly said. 'But what does the rest mean?'

'I don't know, yet. But look!' Josh pointed across the room. On three slender gold plinths stood three small gold sculptures. Olly and Josh walked towards them. One was an ibis – a tall, long-beaked, spindle-legged bird. Its wings were spread wide and its sinuous neck arched down and forwards, supporting a flat golden plate which rested on wing-tips and head.

The next was a sitting cat, slender and elegant with a haughty, Abyssinian face. Between its ears was a strange kind of head-piece – almost like a crown – with a smooth, flattened top.

The last of the golden sculptures was a beetle with a golden dish on its back.

'Two legs, four legs, six legs,' Olly said happily. 'It's them. What about the seven?'

Josh shook his head. He began to circle the room, peering at the etched pictures as they flashed in the guttering light of his failing candle. The wax had burned down almost to his fingers now. It would only be a matter of minutes before he couldn't hold it any more.

Something sparkled in the light. He held the candle closer. There was a pattern of white jewels set into the gold of the wall – seven white diamonds arranged in the same formation as the Pleiades! And about a metre below them was a small golden shelf. 'Bring the statues over here,' Josh called. 'The bird first.'

Olly lifted the heavy golden ibis off its plinth. Josh pointed and she rested it on the shelf.

'Now the cat.'

Olly brought the cat over and placed it on the gold plate on the bird's head. It fitted perfectly. She ran back for the beetle. It sat exactly on the cat's head-piece, the dish on its back in line with the lower stars in the arrangement of diamonds. 'Now what?' she demanded.

'I don't know,' Josh replied. 'It looks as if something should fit into the dish on the beetle's back.' He looked around the room. 'Is there anything else?'

'I don't think so,' Olly responded, also gazing around.

'What else do we have to do?' Josh asked. 'Why hasn't anything happened?' He racked his brains. What had they missed? The three sacred animals had been united under the seven jewels. They had fitted together perfectly. So why weren't the Tears of Isis revealed?

Olly gave a sharp hiss and whipped round to face the doors, which still stood open.

'What is it?' Josh asked.

Olly ran to the doors and peered out. 'I can see torchlight coming this way,' she said. 'It must be Ethan and Mohammed.'

'Close the doors,' Josh instructed.

Olly heaved against the doors and they swung closed with a clang.

Josh winced at the noise. 'If they didn't know we

were here before, they do now,' he remarked.

'I couldn't help it,' Olly snapped, leaning against the doors to hold them shut. 'Get working on the riddle. I'll try and keep the bad guys out.'

Josh stared at the seven jewels. 'The light of the sacred seven,' he muttered under his breath. 'What light? What does it mean?'

Something hit the outside of the doors. The blow vibrated through Olly's back. She flexed her legs, digging her heels in. 'Josh!'

Ethan and Mohammed obviously weren't bothering to look for the release mechanism – they had resorted to brute force.

'Try to find something to wedge the doors shut,' Josh suggested, thinking furiously. He had only one goal – to solve the riddle before the two men burst in. He wasn't thinking about what might happen afterwards.

Boom! Another blow struck the doors.

Olly ran towards the slender plinth that had held the cat statue.

Boom! The doors shuddered.

'What light do they mean?' Josh yelled in frustration.

'Try the candle!' Olly shouted. 'It's the only light we've got.'

Josh thought it was worth a try. He placed the small candle-end in the dish on the scarab's back and stepped away. The flame flickered – for a moment Josh thought it was going to go out. But then it grew stronger, flaring up with a glow as bright as sunlight.

The seven jewels caught the light from the swelling candle flame. They burned with a blinding intensity, their white light building and building as it reflected and rebounded from the polished surfaces of the golden room, until the whole chamber blazed like the sun.

This must be why it's called the Chamber of Light, Josh thought, shielding his eyes with his hand, as a beam of light leapt across the room from the seven jewels to strike a panel in the far wall. A rumbling noise filled the room. He watched in amazement as the golden wall-panel slid back to reveal a recess. There was a statue in the secret alcove – the figure of Isis, made entirely of gold. Her hands were together, palms upwards. And as the light touched them, it scattered into a myriad different colours that bounced and rebounded off the walls, roof and floor, in a dazzling rainbow of light.

At that instant, the doors flew open and Ethan Cain and Mohammed burst into the room. Ethan's eyes were bright and feverish. 'Ah! The Tears of Isis!' he cried. 'At last!'

The two men moved towards the statue of Isis – stumbling directly into the path of the brilliant beam of light. Immediately, they fell back – blinded – trying to protect their eyes.

As Josh stood, frozen in shock, staring at the two men, he saw a movement out of the corner of his eye. Olly held one of the golden plinths in her hands. She swung it and threw it across the room. The heavy golden column spun low through the air and struck Ethan on the shin. He let out a bellow of pain and crumpled to the floor, dragging Mohammed down with him. The Egyptian dropped the torch as he fell and it skidded across the floor towards Josh.

'Come on!' Olly yelled to Josh as she ran to the statue. In her open hands, Isis held a small, golden casket. The lid was open, and inside glittered two enormous pear-shaped blue sapphires. Olly snatched the casket up. As she did so, the lid fell shut, instantly extinguishing the lights. A split second later, Josh's candle flickered and died. The only light now came from Mohammed's torch.

Josh ran forwards and picked up the torch, then he and Olly jumped over the two men and raced for the door.

'Mess with us, huh?' Olly muttered to Ethan as she and Josh pushed the doors shut. 'I don't think so!'

As the doors came together, Josh shone the torch through the crack and caught a last glimpse of Ethan. He was clambering to his feet, his face twisted with pain and anger. He shouted something, but the words were lost behind the clanging doors.

The friends ran – Josh in the lead with the powerful torch, Olly right behind him.

'We need to go back the same way we came!' Josh shouted.

'We'll never find it,' Olly yelled.

Josh realised she was right. The golden room was ringed with avenues of guardian statues. It would take them for ever to find the original path and retrace their steps to the surface – even if they were able to remember the way.

They hurried on through the hall of treasures, until the beam of the torch hit a far wall and revealed a doorway. As they neared the exit tunnel, Olly paused for a moment and looked back over her shoulder.

'What's wrong?' Josh asked.

'Just making sure it's real,' Olly said with a smile.

They emerged into a corridor which sloped gently upwards. Josh and Olly could hear no sounds of pursuit, so they slowed to a brisk walk.

'This must lead somewhere important,' Olly said hopefully, after a while. 'And we're going upwards all the time – that's good news.'

'How far do you think we've come?' Josh asked.

'I don't know,' Olly replied, then stopped for a moment, listening. She shook her head. 'I can't hear anything back there,' she said. She looked at Josh. 'Once we're out, we're going to have to get someone to help us rescue those two. We can't leave them down there without any light.'

Josh nodded. 'But we have to get ourselves out first,' he said. 'Show me the Tears again.'

Olly opened the casket and the sapphires sparkled in the torch light. 'Aren't they fabulous?' she breathed.

'Amazing,' Josh agreed. He grinned. 'I can't wait to show them to Jonathan and your dad.'

'Then we'd better get moving,' Olly said. She shut the casket and the glorious blue light went out.

They walked on. It was several minutes later that Josh saw something ahead of them. A small square of blacker darkness, some way in the distance. He began to walk more quickly. Olly kept up with him and soon they were both running. The square of darkness grew.

They burst out into a large square chamber. The floor was silted and scattered with debris, and the walls were covered in paintings and hieroglyphs. A flight of ten large stone steps led to the roof. The foot of the stairway was guarded by grim shabti warriors of black granite.

Josh shone the torch around the chamber. There didn't seem to be a way out.

'Those steps must be there for a reason,' Olly said, staring up to where the steps met the ceiling of stone blocks. She moved towards the stairway.

'Watch where you walk,' Josh warned her. 'There might be traps.'

Olly slowed down. 'I'll be extra careful,' she said.

At the foot of the stairs she stopped and looked up. 'It seems safe enough,' she murmured and brought one foot down tentatively on the bottom step. She looked over her shoulder at Josh. 'It's fine,' she told him. But as she put her weight on the step, it slid downwards a few centimetres with a grating sound. 'Oh, please – no. Not another booby-trap!' Olly breathed.

A low rumble sounded from above her head. Josh shone the torch upwards. Sand was filtering down from between the cracks in the stone roof. Loud grating and grinding sounds now filled the chamber. 'Move!' Josh shouted.

Sand began to cascade down, with small stones that bounced on the steps and struck Olly on her head and shoulders. She threw herself backwards as a large block came crashing down, striking the stairs and breaking them as it tumbled to the floor. In its wake, sand and rubble cascaded out of the rift in the ceiling.

'Olly!' Josh shouted in panic, as his friend screamed and vanished from sight – hidden by the flood of debris that poured from the broken ceiling and rushed in a torrent down the steps.

Chapter Fourteen

The Tears of Isis

Dust billowed in thick grey clouds, clogging Olly's lungs and sending her reeling backwards as the roof of the chamber fell in.

'Olly!' she heard Josh shout, but her mouth was thick with grit and she couldn't reply. She scrambled into a corner of the chamber and rolled herself into a protective ball as dirt and stones showered down over her. She expected to be crushed at any moment by a falling stone block.

But it didn't happen. The noise lessened and the surge of debris dwindled to a trickle of sand and pebbles. She took her arms away from her head and stared upwards. At first she couldn't understand what she was seeing. It looked like dark blue velvet scattered with diamonds. It must be another ceiling, she thought, above the chamber roof – painted to look like the night sky.

A breath of air touched her cheek. Her vision cleared and the roof of stars suddenly leapt away into the far, far distance. She realised that she was gazing up at the sky – the *real* night sky!

'We did it!' she breathed. 'We escaped!'

She looked across the chamber for Josh. The clouds of dust were thinning and she saw him pressed against the far wall, staring at her in shocked relief.

'I thought you'd got yourself killed!' he said.

Olly grinned. 'Not me,' she replied. But she was only too aware of how lucky she had been. The booby-trap had clearly been set to catch anyone climbing the stairs. The fact that she had thrown herself backwards, away from the steps, had saved her life.

Josh came over to help Olly to her feet. Together, they climbed over the wreckage and scrambled up the stairs.

'Fresh air!' Olly said. 'Can you smell it?'

'Yes,' Josh replied with a happy sigh.

Earth and sand sloped up to ground level about

a metre above their heads. It was late evening and the very last rays of the sun were smouldering beyond the western mountains.

'I wonder where we are,' Olly said.

The crater hole was several metres across. They began to climb out.

'Olivia! Josh! What on earth is going on? How did you get down there?' came a familiar voice from above.

'Gran?' Olly said in surprise. Her head came up above ground level and she instantly saw where she and Josh had surfaced. They were in front of the trailers – not far from the table and chairs. Natasha Welles and Audrey Beckmann were gazing down into the chasm that had opened up almost under their feet.

'Josh!' Natasha gasped.

'I'm OK, Mum,' Josh called.

Mrs Beckmann stared into the hole. 'What sort of stupid games have you been up to?' she demanded as she helped Olly out. 'You could have been killed! And if you've caused any damage down there your father will never forgive you.'

Natasha offered a helping hand to Josh, looking at the two dishevelled friends in astonished disbelief.

Olly grasped her gran's hands, her face glowing. 'It's huge down there, Gran – bigger than you'd ever believe,' Olly explained. 'We found the room that devours itself. But Ethan and Mohammed were chasing us. They're still down there, and—'

'What are you talking about?' her gran interrupted. She frowned at Josh. 'What is all this nonsense?'

'She's telling the truth,' Josh said. 'Ethan wants the Tears for himself.' He looked at his mother. 'I'm sorry, Mum, but it's true. We need to find Jonathan and the professor.'

Natasha looked completely bewildered. 'Surely they're still down in the tomb,' she said. She frowned at Josh. 'I don't understand – what was that about Ethan?'

Olly impulsively gave her gran a hug. 'I've got so much to tell you,' she said. 'But right now I have to find Dad.' She drew back and pulled the golden casket out of her pocket. 'You see, we've found the Tears of Isis!' And with that, she broke away from her gran and raced towards the main entrance of the tomb. Josh chased after her.

The two stunned women looked at one another for a moment, and then they, too, began to run towards the tomb of Setiankhra.

Olly and Josh tumbled into the burial chamber, just as Jonathan and Professor Christie were climbing out through the secret doorway.

'You're safe!' Olly exclaimed happily. 'I was afraid they might have hurt you.'

'Olly, marvellous news!' exclaimed the professor. 'We've found the sarcophagus of Setiankhra!' He gestured towards the doorway. 'It's in a chamber through there. It's the most wonderful thing!'

Jonathan looked at the two friends. 'What happened to you?' he asked, staring at their grimy faces and dirty clothes. '*Who* might have hurt us?'

'Ethan and Mohammed,' Josh told him.

Olly ran forwards. 'And Dad, we've found the Tears!'

Both men stared at her incredulously. Olly held the golden casket out on the palm of her hand and raised the lid. The beautiful sapphires glittered and shone. Jonathan and the professor drew closer, gazing at the jewels.

'What is this, Olivia?' the professor breathed. 'Where did you find these?'

'In the room that devours itself!' Olly replied, grinning.

187

'Which way did you turn when you went through the secret door?' Josh asked.

'To the right,' Jonathan told him.

Olly shook her head. 'Wrong way,' she said. 'We went left – and you're not going to believe what we found!'

'But we have to warn you about Ethan and Mohammed,' Josh said.

'*What* about them?' Jonathan asked.

At that moment, Natasha and Audrey Beckmann came running breathlessly into the chamber.

'They're criminals!' Josh said. He glanced at his mother. 'Both of them! Ethan was behind the theft of the Elephantine Stone. Mohammed was helping him.' He pointed towards the secret door. 'They chased us in there. It's a long story, but we managed to get their torch and find our way out.'

Natasha stared at him in disbelief. 'This is insane,' she said. 'Ethan isn't a *criminal*.'

Jonathan looked hard at Josh. 'Are they still down there without any light?' he asked sharply.

'Yes,' Olly nodded. 'We left them in the Chamber of Light.'

Josh opened his mouth to speak, but Jonathan silenced him with a gesture of his hand. He looked at Professor Christie. 'We need to get in there and find them,' he said.

'Ethan!' Natasha suddenly exclaimed.

Everyone followed the direction of her gaze. She was looking at the secret door and Ethan Cain was there, doubled over, one hand against the wall. His clothes were dirty and torn and there was a raw, bloody graze on his cheek. Blood trailed from the corner of his mouth and his lips were swollen and bruised.

'Help me,' he panted, almost falling into the room. Jonathan and Natasha ran forwards to catch him. He seemed dizzy and breathless. 'Mohammed,' he murmured. 'You have to stop Mohammed before he gets away. He stole the Elephantine Stone!'

'Don't trust him!' Olly shouted. 'Mohammed was working for him.'

Ethan stared at her in surprise. 'That's not true,' he protested. 'I tried to stop him.' He gestured to his face. 'He did this to me.'

'No,' Josh said, glaring at Ethan. 'You were working together to steal the Tears of Isis.'

Ethan shook his head. He pulled himself upright with a visible effort. 'I let Mohammed think I'd help him steal the stone.' He looked at Professor Christie. 'I thought I could get him to reveal himself if I played along with him,' he said. 'I was stupid. When I confronted him, he went crazy. I thought he was going to kill me.'

'That's not true, Dad,' Olly said. 'He's lying to you!'

Ethan coughed weakly. 'No, Olly, really I'm not,' he insisted.

'Then why were you chasing us?' Josh demanded.

'Mohammed was determined to go after you,' Ethan said. 'I couldn't risk letting him hurt you. So, I went with him.'

'That's not how it happened!' Olly exclaimed in exasperation.

Ethan smiled kindly at her. 'I don't blame you for being confused, Olly, but I'm telling the truth. There was a long chase through the dark.' He glanced up at the professor. 'It's immense down there – dozens of rooms and probably miles of corridors. It's a stupendous find!'

'So I've heard,' said the professor. 'But what about Mohammed?'

Ethan frowned. 'Well, we found Olly and Josh in a golden room,' he said. 'There was a bright light which completely dazzled me. I couldn't see a thing. Then something struck my legs and I stumbled into Mohammed. We both fell. Before either of us could get up, Olly and Josh had taken our torch and gone. Mohammed was crazy with anger. I could tell he was prepared to hurt Olly and Josh to get the Tears from them. I tried to reason with him, but he attacked me. He had another, smaller torch, so he left me there on the floor and went after Olly and Josh. It was a few minutes before I could walk.' He shook his head. 'I tried to follow him, but I couldn't see which way he had gone. In the end I used my cigar lighter to find my way out.' Ethan pulled free from Natasha and Jonathan. 'But we must find Mohammed now,' he said anxiously. 'There's no time to lose!'

'You're far too badly hurt,' Natasha argued. 'We need to get you to a doctor.'

'You don't actually believe his story, do you?' Olly exclaimed.

Natasha frowned at her. 'Stop it, Olly!' she snapped. 'Ethan's right – you're just confused.' She looked at Josh and her voice softened. 'Who wouldn't be after what you've been through? But Ethan got hurt trying to protect you, can't you see that?'

Josh stared speechlessly at his mother.

Olly was lost for words, too. She looked from face to face and realised that no one believe their story. Ethan had won everyone over.

'It doesn't matter,' Ethan said, smiling weakly at the two friends. 'It was all a misunderstanding.' He took a step towards them. 'But I have to know one thing – did you find the Tears of Isis?'

Olly stared at him. He was so persuasive that for a moment she almost believed him. But then she remembered the ferocious look of greed she had seen on his face in the Chamber of Light. However, she knew it was pointless to carry on accusing him when everyone else was convinced that she and Josh were just mistaken. Looking coldly into his face, she showed him the Tears of Isis.

Ethan's eyes gleamed as he gazed at the fabulous jewels. 'Beautiful,' he said. He looked round at the professor. 'Congratulations, Professor. There are chambers of treasure back there,' he said. 'This is the greatest find since Tutankhamen – possibly the greatest untouched hoard ever discovered in Egypt! You're going to be famous.'

'That can wait,' said Mrs Beckmann, taking charge of the situation. 'First, we need to call the police to tell them about Mohammed. Jonathan – deal with that, please. Natasha and I will take Ethan to my caravan. He can rest there and we'll clean him up and see how much damage has been done.' She turned to the youngsters. 'Olivia, you can help us. Josh – I'd like you to run over to the diggers' camp. Wake a few of them up and tell them the professor needs them immediately.' She looked at the professor. 'They can mount an overnight guard on the place, just in case Mohammed is still in the vicinity.'

While Olly was still reeling from the turn of events, her father stepped up to her and lifted the casket out of her hands. 'These need to be put somewhere safe,' he said, closing the lid. 'Go with your gran now, Olivia. We'll study the Tears of Isis tomorrow.'

Olly stared at Josh, stunned by the way the adults had taken over and by how easily Ethan had fooled them all.

Josh gave her a blank, helpless look that showed he was feeling the same way. Then he turned and ran off on the errand that Olly's gran had given him.

* * *

It was a busy night. The police arrived with some bad news of their own. Benjamin Carter was gone – he had bribed a guard and escaped from his cell. A hunt was on, but so far there had been no sign of him.

Police officers examined Mohammed's tent, but found it stripped of his possessions. He had beaten them to it. The laptop – the final shred of evidence that Olly and Josh had hoped might link Ethan Cain to the theft of the Elephantine Stone – was gone.

And the man himself seemed to have melted away into the desert night. The police promised to do all they could to track him down, but they didn't seem hopeful. One officer stayed at the site to keep watch over the tomb.

Professor Christie didn't enter the tomb again that night. He spent the evening in his trailer, making calls to Cairo University and the Egyptian authorities, informing them of the find, and inviting them to join him in exploring the extraordinary lost catacombs of Setiankhra's tomb.

It was midnight before the camp began to settle down. Beds were found for Natasha and Ethan.

The golden casket that contained the Tears of Isis was locked away in the security box, and Jonathan slept with it by his side.

Neither Josh nor Olly found it easy to sleep. Olly lay wide-eyed far into the night, torn between the almost unbearable excitement of their discovery, and her deep dismay that Ethan Cain had fooled everyone. At least his schemes failed and we beat him to the Tears of Isis, she told herself. And comforted by that thought, she eventually drifted into a shallow, restless sleep.

It seemed only a few minutes later that Olly was woken by somebody shaking her shoulder. She snuggled deeper under the covers. 'Go away, Josh,' she mumbled. 'You're such a pain!'

'Olivia!' It was her gran's voice. 'Wake up, now, love.'

Olly forced her eyes open. Audrey Beckmann was leaning over her.

'What time is it?' Olly asked.

'It's still early, but Natasha and Ethan are leaving shortly. I thought you'd want to see them off. I've already woken Josh.'

Olly was suddenly wide awake. 'I thought Ethan

was staying till the helicopter was fixed,' she said as she hopped out of bed.

'Change of plans,' said her gran, picking up Olly's clothes from the floor and handing them to her. 'They're both catching a flight from Luxor airport this morning. Apparently, there's some kind of problem at Ethan's head office and he has to deal with it personally.' She frowned. 'How many times have I told you not to throw your things all over the floor when you get undressed?'

Olly was climbing into her clothes. 'Sorry, Gran,' she said.

Her gran sat down at the end of her bed. 'Now, Olly,' she began. 'I don't want any more nonsense about Ethan.' She raised a warning finger. 'Make sure you're on your best behaviour – and be quick, now.' She got up, patted Olly on the back and left the room.

Olly frowned. Best behaviour! If only her gran knew what had *really* happened down in Setiankhra's tomb. But she didn't, and that was that. Olly sighed. At least she and Josh had found the Tears and wrecked Ethan's plans. She'd remember that when she had to wave him goodbye.

Natasha and Ethan were ready to leave by the time Olly appeared. One of the diggers was going to drive them to the airport in the Land Rover. Jonathan, Josh, Audrey Beckmann and the professor were saying their farewells to the glamorous couple as Olly came up.

'Well, it's been quite a visit, hasn't it?' Natasha said, giving Olly a hug.

Olly smiled. 'I'll say.' She exchanged a knowing look with Josh.

Ethan turned towards the two friends. 'No hard feelings about our little misunderstanding,' he said, smiling cheerfully at them. 'You should both be very proud,' he continued. 'You've discovered something that other people have spent entire lifetimes searching for. I only wish I could spare the time to explore the tomb with you.'

Olly looked steadily into his eyes and smiled sweetly. 'Why do you have to go?' she asked. 'Couldn't you stay a little while longer?' She knew the real reason he had changed his plans – now that the Tears were safely under lock and key he had no hope of getting his hands on them.

Ethan met her gaze. 'Business has to come first,' he sighed. He leant towards her, smiling. 'But I'll

197

be following your father's quest for the other Talismans of the Moon with great interest,' he told her. 'And you never know – I may even find time to visit you now and then and see how you're all getting on.'

Olly stared at him – for a moment she caught a glint in his eyes that wasn't at all friendly. Then he turned and climbed into the Land Rover with a final wave.

The little group watched and waved as the Land Rover headed down towards the river.

'Did you see that look he gave me?' Olly whispered to Josh.

'Yes,' Josh whispered back. 'And I didn't like that comment about watching your father's search for the other talismans with "great interest"!'

'Me neither,' Olly agreed. 'I'm sure we haven't seen the last of him. But we beat him this time, and if he comes back for more, we'll just have to beat him again.'

'What are you two whispering about?' Mrs Beckmann asked.

'Nothing, Gran,' Olly replied lightly. 'When's breakfast?'

* * *

It was shortly after breakfast that the first of the visitors arrived on site. Professor Khalil Fehr, Head of Egyptology at Cairo University, was a tall, courteous man with grey hair and a face as brown and wrinkled as a walnut. He brought with him a team of archaeologists and scientists who had flown in to examine the great discoveries. Professor Christie was in his element among so many experts on ancient Egypt. Soon he was lost in conversation and debate with his eminent colleagues.

Olly was desperate to go down into the tomb again. She couldn't understand why it was taking so long for her father to get round to it.

'A lot of important people need to be involved,' her gran explained. 'We're visitors in this country, Olivia, remember that. Your father wants to do this properly.'

Over the next hour, various Egyptian dignitaries and government officials began to arrive from Luxor, Aswan and Cairo. They greeted Professor Christie enthusiastically, congratulating him on his find, all of them eager to see the ancient treasures that had been discovered.

'It's not me you have to thank,' the professor told them all modestly. 'My daughter, Olivia, and her friend, Josh, made the most astonishing finds.'

At last, everyone gathered around the hole through which Olly and Josh had escaped the tomb the previous night. Jonathan had been up since shortly after dawn, supervising a team of diggers who had worked to make the hole safe. The roof was now shored up with timbers, and more steps had been added to make the descent into the chamber easier.

'This is not the method by which we first entered the tomb,' the professor explained. 'But the other route is rather more difficult and dangerous.'

'I'll say,' muttered Olly, thinking of the skeletons.

'Shh!' hissed Josh. 'He's talking about us!'

'My daughter and Josh are the ones who actually found the Chamber of Light and the Tears of Isis,' the professor was saying.

All eyes turned to the two friends. Olly grinned and seemed to glow with pride, while Josh, embarrassed by so much attention, endeavoured to hide behind his shaggy blond hair.

'We will now enter the tomb of Setiankhra,' Professor Christie continued. 'And I would like Olly and Josh to be our guides.'

Olly and Josh stared at each other in astonishment – neither of them had expected this.

'You're the only ones who know the way,' Jonathan pointed out to them quietly, smiling at their shocked expressions.

The friends soon recovered from their surprise, and side by side, they led the way down into the catacombs of Setiankhra's tomb.

As they made their way through the spectacular hall of treasures, they heard gasps of amazement from the group behind them. Josh looked at Olly and grinned.

'I can see that being heroic explorers is going to take up an awful lot of our time,' Olly said to him thoughtfully.

Josh nodded. 'You're right. I mean, we still have all the other Talismans of the Moon to find, for a start. I don't know when we'll be able to fit in schoolwork.'

A determined look crossed Olly's face. 'I don't think eminent explorers should have to do schoolwork, anyway,' she said firmly.

Josh chuckled. 'I can't wait to hear you explain that to your gran,' he told her.

They had reached the golden doors at the heart

of the hall of treasures. Here they stopped and turned to the party of archaeologists. 'Ladies and gentlemen,' Olly announced. 'Welcome to the Chamber of Light!'

And as she and Josh moved forwards again, the great golden doors swung smoothly open.

The Mooncake of Chang-O

Olly Christie and Josh Welles are travelling the world with Olly's father, Professor Christie, on a search for the precious Talismans of the Moon. But danger lurks in the shadows. Can Josh and Olly outwit whoever is trying to get there first?

Olly and Josh are in China on the track of another precious talisman – the Mooncake of Chang-O. Once again the friends' eager investigations lead them into all sorts of trouble – escaping an ancient sect, finding a lost city and outwitting a dangerous enemy who wants the talisman for himself . . .